In Memory of Phyllis Stancill Pruden

My mother told the shy teenager she should be a newspaper reporter.
Years later, my mother told the investigative reporter she should write
a book. Thank you, Mother, for sensing things about me I couldn't
see. Wish you could read my fourth book.

Love,
Nancy

"Crackling with immediacy and suspense, *Deadly Secrets* is an unforgettable political thriller about murder, corruption and personal freedom in the divided states of America.

Welcome to Westcarolina, the newest American state. Encompassing a conservative region of what was once western North Carolina, the new government is sponsored and backed by Kingston Avery, the state's minister-governor. The move follows a pattern happening elsewhere. Secessionists in Texas are... enroute to becoming a true nation, and similar movements are also underway in Alaska and California.

As *Deadly Secrets* opens, a radicalized anti-abortion activist and his wife are about to become domestic terrorists. Specifically, they bomb a local chemical plant that makes a key ingredient of the abortion pill. The act appears to have the full backing of God's Gift leadership, of which they are insiders.

Enter 42-year-old Pulitzer-prize winning report Annie Price. After accepting a new job offer, she travels to Westcarolina to cover the new state. Little does she know that one of Avery's top officials, Rob Ryland, is responsible for murdering her best friend back in Texas.

Annie quickly sets about interviewing residents, community leaders and politicians... As she continues to dig into what appears to be an unconstitutional theocracy in the making, a series of troubling "accidents" begin to claim the lives of Avery's rivals--and even some of his allies.

...The book can be read as pure entertainment but given how closely the book parallels real political divisions, it's equally effective as a warning."
–BestThrillers

"Investigative journalist Annie Price is at it again in *Deadly Secrets*. When a church-led secessionist movement pushes the envelope, someone must dig deep to find the truth. Well-written with a strong female protagonist, *Deadly Secrets* employs themes of greed, religious takeovers, and political turmoil, yet is balanced with those of love, trust, and personal growth. A must-read for fans of good reporting and twisted characters."
–Kathryn Dare, *Portland Book Review*

AN ANNIE PRICE MYSTERY

DEADLY SECRETS

NANCY STANCILL

Black Rose Writing | Texas

ISBN: 978-1-68513-524-9
PUBLISHED BY BLACK ROSE WRITING
www.blackrosewriting.com

Printed in the United States of America
Suggested Retail Price (SRP) $19.95

Deadly Secrets is printed in Adobe Caslon Pro

"Nancy Stancill has done it again! Annie Price--the investigative reporter felled by gunshot wounds while investigating successionists and baby-selling schemes in Texas--has recovered and brought her considerable talents to Charlotte, North Carolina where she tangles with Christian fundamentalists who aren't afraid to kill, and the equally dangerous leadership of a new ultra-conservative state called Westcarolina. . . Events pile on events, the pace is quick, and you'll find yourself turning pages long after your bedtime."
–David Collins, author of *Accidental Activists, Mark Phariss, Vic Holmes, and their Fight for Marriage Equality in Texas;* and editor of *Boundless*

"Imagine western North Carolina has seceded from the state to become a theocracy where the explosive schemes of its evangelical leader and his hypocritical minions gain the attention of seasoned investigative reporter, Annie Price. From the big city lights of Charlotte to the mountain resort town of Blowing Rock, with stops along the way for pork barbeque, hush puppies, banana pudding, and other Southern tastes, Annie has a lot on her plate as surprising events in her love life intersect with a dangerous political world turned upside down."
–Landis Wade, founder, Charlotte Readers Podcast, and author of *Deadly Declarations*

"A sharp, page-turning mystery that left me breathless as journalist Annie Price untangles shady business deals, a bombing, and a series of murders connected to Westcarolina, a new "Christian state" created from a section of North Carolina. The reporter is unexpectedly charmed by the new governor but horrified when someone from her past emerges in a major leadership position."
–Donna Koros Stramella, author of *Coffee Killed My Mother* and *Among the Bones*

"Libraries and readers seeking a story set in a fictional, yet familiar, near future where religious, psychological, social, and political interests intersect will find much to appreciate in Annie's character and focus in *Deadly Secrets*.

Book clubs, too, will find it an unexpected opportunity to discuss a variety of subjects about church, state, women's issues, and the price of proactive thinking and behavior on all sides.

In short: *Deadly Secrets* is powerful in its characterizations, astute in its political extrapolations, unexpected in its action and twists and turns, and hard to put down."
–D. Donovan, editor, *Bookwatch*

ACKNOWLEDGEMENTS

Writing a novel is solitary and difficult, worrisome and deflating, and ultimately, rewarding and triumphant.

Then the real fun begins. Showing it to friends and writing colleagues, getting their feedback, and expressing your appreciation for their efforts is a pleasure.

This is my fourth book and a continuation of my Annie Price, investigative reporter, series. It's my second book edited by the talented and generous Steve Johnston, with a heavy assist by devoted reader Len Norman.

I want to thank friends and fellow writers for their careful reading and comments, including Dannye Powell, Don Mason, Claudia Feldman, Leslie Gerber, Julia Edmunds, Karen Garloch, Pam Kelley, and Judy Tell. A special shoutout goes to Daniel Norman, my writer friend and brother-in-law, for his constant encouragement.

My undying gratitude goes to my writing group members–Kelly Bennett, Chris Daly, Erika Lopez, Karen McDermott, Molly McDermott, Dorothy Trotter, Susan Whatmore, Jonathan Heaslet, and our wonderful leader, Maureen Ryan Griffin. Though the composition of the group may change from time to time, its support never wavers.

A special thank you to my dear family, husband Len Norman; son Jeffrey Norman; and beloved siblings, Diane Hall; Melinda Poe; Steve Stancill; and Jane Stancill. They are always there for me, as are their wonderful family members.

Lastly, my sincere gratitude to Reagan Rothe, founder and CEO of Black Rose Writing, and his excellent staff, for believing in my books for ten years.

And as many authors say, any mistakes are mine.

DEADLY SECRETS

CHAPTER 1

Stealthily and carefully, Rad Montgomery maneuvered the pickup truck into a space beside the Lenogue Chemicals factory. He was determined to bomb the facility but wondered if he'd still be alive in an hour.

The long Lenogue building, brick with few windows and an inconspicuous sign, was in a rural area near Gastonia, Westcarolina. Inside, one product manufactured was top secret, even from the workers.

The plant produced mifepristone, a key ingredient in the abortion pill. The factory supplied enough mifepristone to make pills for medication abortions in most of the southern states.

Rad and his wife, Ceil, who was in a stolen getaway car less than a mile away, abhorred abortion. They knew that nearly two-thirds of the U.S. terminations each year were medication abortions using the abortion pill. Those numbers were growing, thanks to the Supreme Court decision reversing Roe vs. Wade. The abortion pill was also under siege. Bombing the factory would reduce the national supply.

Before Rad knew how to construct explosives, he and Ceil protested at abortion clinics throughout the country. The Internet taught him how to make bombs that were progressively more deadly.

Rad used his national contacts in the pro-life movement to find sensitive information. It was a fluke that he'd learned the Lenogue factory might make the abortion ingredient. Rad and Ceil's secret plan to destroy the plant thrilled more extreme leaders of the anti-abortion movement. It was midnight, time for action. The bombs in the truck would destroy the building and could kill or wound a couple of guards. Rad believed that, while unfortunate, that was an acceptable tradeoff.

After making sure everything was ready, Rad ran from the truck to the stolen car, parked a half-mile away. Ceil gunned it and they sped away. He experienced relief–and almost surprise–that he had survived the setup.

"Any problems?" she asked.

"Not so far. Everything was as smooth as silk. Didn't see a guard, but there might be a couple inside the plant."

When they heard the explosion, they exchanged triumphant smiles.

"Another godly mission accomplished," Ceil said. "You're a marvel, my dear."

"So are you, sweetheart. We're a great team."

Rad thought about how lucky he was to have Ceil. They'd been together for twenty years, and rarely argued about anything. Their politics and philosophies about life meshed completely.

Rad considered Ceil a soulmate, never more when they could work together on something worthy, like the factory bombing.

She headed to their modest Charlotte apartment to retrieve their fierce German Shepherd, Trumpet. From Charlotte, they'd hurry to a safe house in the mountains.

The Montgomerys were a couple in their mid-forties. Ceil was full-figured–beautifully filled out, Rad thought–and usually wore jeans and running shoes. Rad was thin, with a well-trimmed beard, and favored a slightly preppy look. They had no children. If he was being truthful, Rad would admit he disliked being around kids, disdaining the disruption created by friends' children. Luckily, he'd married a woman who felt the same way.

Rad referred to the two of them as the Westcarolina Righteous Action Committee. He considered their ministry an informal part of God's Gift Church. Kingston Avery, the leader of the mega-church, was the sponsor and guiding force behind the creation of a new state called Westcarolina.

A year ago, the Montgomerys had wandered into one of God's Gift church's services and found themselves hooked. Rad had offered their specialized services to Avery, and he quietly introduced them to rich anti-abortion couples who could help. He told them he couldn't be directly involved and never to mention his name or that of the church.

Rad Montgomery's idol was Eric Rudolph, an American terrorist who bombed Atlanta's Olympic Park during the 1996 Summer Olympics in the city. Before authorities caught him hiding in Western North Carolina in 2003, Rudolph had bombed two abortion clinics and a lesbian nightclub.

Though Rudolph was now serving four consecutive life sentences for killing two people and injuring more than one hundred, Rad's admiration was absolute.

In due time, Rad thought most Americans, particularly those in Westcarolina, would be passionately pro-life.

CHAPTER 2

The Rev. Kingston Avery was secretly pleased.

The plan to rid much of the United States of medical abortions by blowing up the Lenogue plant was an unqualified success. The expert bombers, the Montgomerys, had completed their work without being caught.

Like much of his congregation, King opposed abortion, but he rarely preached against it. Even in his evangelical church, there were differing viewpoints. He didn't want it to become a bone of contention when there were plenty of other simmering issues. It would affect his healthy level of donations. In addition, he didn't want to be publicly associated with a bombing that'd killed two guards.

When three wealthy church couples had come to him wanting radical action on abortion, he introduced them to Rad and Ceil. He let the donors and would-be bombers mostly plan the operation themselves. But he pulled a few strings in the background, as he usually did on most things.

King was spending most of his time setting up his new state of Westcarolina. He silently corrected himself. The state wasn't exactly his, but he'd be its leader and inspiration.

King was 41 and had been at the top of the evangelical Christian scene in North Carolina for ten years. His God's Gift ministry was a true mega-church, with thousands of members and a dozen locations throughout Charlotte and Gastonia. Most congregations met in schools or large, leased buildings, but he'd built three especially opulent churches designed to look like medieval fortresses. In recent years, he'd begun to expand westward.

He wasn't an especially introspective man, but occasionally took stock of his life. His thoughts wandered as he sat in his Charlotte office, a light-filled space with black leather furniture and an antique desk.

He knew that a big reason that his God's Gift churches flourished was his effect on women. King was tall with longish blonde hair, an aquiline nose and a muscled runner's build. When he took the pulpit to urge his congregations to support God's Gift ministries, his blazing blue eyes flashed with a passion some women rarely saw in their humdrum lives.

King had a fondness for beautiful women, but he seldom engaged in extramarital affairs. He didn't find other women interesting enough to take the chance of sullying his reputation as a man of the cloth. He and his wife Claire, a woman who'd inherited millions of dollars from her banker father, lived together mostly peacefully, he thought. But for a long time, they'd operated under an open marriage arrangement.

Claire had embraced the concept with a vengeance, with no trouble finding new boyfriends who relieved her boredom with life. King didn't quite understand why Claire couldn't stay faithful to him, seemed unhappy most of the time and refused to even consider having children. He'd married her in his early twenties, when he was madly in love with the beautiful, intelligent woman. But after the honeymoon period was over, she'd made known her dissatisfaction with him, and her new life. He was bitterly disappointed, but he tolerated the new arrangement. He could survive a divorce because of his popularity as the top church official, but Claire didn't want one.

Claire was five years older than King and occasionally made available a fraction of her inherited money to support the church's special projects. She'd grown up wealthy and controlled her fortune with an iron fist.

Depending on funds raised from church and business sources was his primary way of supporting his ministry. He had used some millions of dollars his churches collected annually from members to diversify its holdings, which included real estate and businesses. He pretended to invest heavily in impoverished areas, such as some countries in Africa, but that was mostly window dressing for his secular ventures.

While most of the money went to benefit the church, he kept a generous cut for himself. He told himself there was nothing wrong with that. He kept his salary relatively low to avoid pesky questions and secretly saved other money for a rainy day–or an escape to the Caribbean, if needed.

He and Claire owned a high-rise condo in uptown Charlotte, but their principal residence was a twelve-bedroom mansion near the resort town of Blowing Rock. King loved the big estate and used it for most of his office work and the occasional parties he and Claire hosted there. Their parties were legendary but confined mostly to the largest givers within the God's Gift congregations. His supporters knew to keep quiet about some activities at the parties–or face social oblivion by not being invited back.

King had decided to become a minister when he was just a boy, after watching his grandfather preach in the evangelical church he'd founded. Even as a child, he'd studied his grandfather carefully. What made him so successful with people?

When he was ten, his grandfather put him on stage for one of his revivals. The church members loved the blond-haired boy, whose sweet voice trembled with conviction. Thereafter, his grandfather started including King in all his services. His popularity was stunning. He graduated from college after majoring in theology and immediately started working for his grandfather. His parents, a welder and a homemaker who weren't particularly religious, were mostly indifferent to his choice. They trusted his grandfather to take care of him.

It wasn't his powerful belief in God that led him to start his own evangelical ministry in his mid-twenties. In fact, doubts that God even existed tormented him, though he hid them well. It was the promise of power and riches that brought him to his profession. Despite his wild success in creating a dozen church branches in

Charlotte and Gastonia, he often experienced a sense of emptiness. He wondered why he couldn't believe with the fervor of his grandfather, or the way he'd felt as a child. He thought of himself as a fraud, preaching the gospel that he thought was rife with strange stories and contradictions. Maybe it was his mother who'd steered him away from his naïve beliefs. She had little respect for her father-in-law's ministry, which she thought preyed on the poor and stupid.

His inclination towards politics outweighed his interest in religion, and he knew it. Over ten years, he'd thrown his support behind prominent state and national Republicans from the conservative wing. He'd shown his loyalty to a select few national figures who'd won races that surprised everyone. He contributed generously to the most influential politician and the two men became close friends. King had felt confident in telling the popular figure what he really wanted—a section of North Carolina that he could mold to suit his evangelical flock—and business interests. The top leader had obliged with an executive order supporting the secession.

Splitting a large area from an existing state had gone more smoothly than he'd visualized. After the Republican-controlled state legislature had voted yes on cleaving North Carolina in two, the issue went to Congress. Both Houses approved it after some contentious debate. It was the prospect of two new likely conservative senators and a few new House members—depending on lines drawn—that galvanized the Republican vote. A few Democrats joined in, because they knew that Westcarolina was attracting new residents from other parts of the country all the time and would probably become more liberal as time went by.

King had grown up in Western North Carolina and felt it was ideal for his purposes. The western part of the state presently consisted mostly of white religious and social conservatives, his people. He'd act quickly to tamp down the few liberal areas, including Asheville.

The entrance of Henry Fullspear, vice president of God's Gift Ministries, interrupted his thoughts. King's second-in-command, 56, took charge of directing the many financial activities of the empire.

Henry didn't look or act like a minister. He was medium tall with graying hair, Harry Potter-style glasses and a voice that didn't carry. King counted on his loyalty that sometimes included doing things that were quasi-legal, at best. It was too bad, he thought, that he could barely stand being around his second-in-command. He couldn't put a single reason on his feelings, but Henry was just obnoxious—too loud and overly confident. Maybe it was because he had grown up in the West, an area that seemed alien to King. He'd met Henry at a theological conference ten years ago and despite his off-putting personality, he'd heard that the older man was a whiz at handling money. After he'd hired Henry, he'd found that his second-in-command was hopeless as a preacher. He stayed in the background, which suited King just fine.

"Boss, we made it," Henry said in his too-excited voice. "The North Carolina legislature appointed you to a two-year term as governor of Westcarolina, which they praised as a new Christian state. I'm to be lieutenant governor."

King, who'd worked hard to lobby the conservatives in the legislature, felt disappointed.

"Just two years?"

"After that, you can run for a four-year term."

"That's more like it," King said. He peppered Henry with questions. "Did North Carolina agree to share some of its resources with Westcarolina? Did you tell them that we don't have time yet to set up agencies like the highway patrol? Do they know we can augment some of their agencies with funding and staffing until we have our own? We'll have to negotiate carefully, which I'm sure you'll do."

"Oh, yeah. They seem agreeable to discussing anything."

"Are they concerned about the lawsuits against the state?" King asked. Several entities had sued North Carolina, including several

Western N.C. groups, Democratic party leaders and the American Civil Liberties Union, contending that Westcarolina was illegally seceding to give conservatives more power.

"No, they're pooh-poohing the suits. They're confident that conservative judges will dismiss them—and you know how many conservative judges serve in North Carolina."

The two men bumped fists, and King finally rewarded him with a small smile.

"Everything we've worked for is falling into place," Henry said.

CHAPTER 3

Annie Price was running, running, running, but she couldn't outrun the woman with the pistol. She heard two loud bangs and saw, to her horror, the blood pouring from her side and arm.

Startled from her sleep, she woke with a loud cry, her body covered in sweat and filled with tension. She'd had a nightmare based on memory. Juliana Souza, a Houston woman of Brazilian descent operating a baby scam in the Texas Hill Country, had shot her a year earlier.

Souza had coerced 36 immigrant women from several countries to become pregnant with donated semen by blackmailing them or promising green cards. She could sell their babies to desperate couples willing to pay upwards of $70,000 for each infant.

Annie, then a reporter for the *Houston Times*, had uncovered the scheme. She had secretly traveled to the remote ranch where the women were held prisoner and interviewed some of them. She was trying to leave when Souza discovered and shot her. Souza had escaped, probably to Brazil. Authorities had convicted her Houston boyfriend and partner in the illegal venture on multiple charges, resulting in a lengthy prison term.

Annie had always wanted to be an investigative reporter and had sometimes found herself in dangerous situations. But she had experienced no physical harm until she'd uncovered the baby scam a year ago. She'd taken a long time to recover from the wounds, both physical and psychological. She was mostly fine now, but occasionally the nightmares still came.

Annie was ready to work again, but the management had turned her beloved newspaper into a smaller print edition with a breezy website. The *Times* had also laid off some strong reporters. A paper that welcomed investigative reporting and had a well-regarded print product, along with a good website, was what she wanted. She'd come to the Houston newspaper from a smaller paper in Virginia a few years after graduating from the University of North Carolina. Getting the job at the *Houston Times* had thrilled her, and she had worked her way up from reporting at one bureau to the investigative reporting desk.

At 42, she feared starting over, though she'd had a few job overtures while recuperating. None had sounded interesting or were in places she might enjoy living. But her savings were dwindling, and she needed to find something soon.

It was still early, but she got up anyway and made a pot of coffee. After she'd fed her two yowling cats, Benjy and Marbles, she sprawled on the living room sofa with her laptop. She started her day by looking at websites for the *New York Times* and the *Washington Post*. Today they both had bare-bones stories of an explosion at a large abortion pill plant in Westcarolina, the new state. She read to the end of the stories, surprised and intrigued.

She called up the website of the *Charlotte Press*, which also had a breaking story on the explosion that'd happened late the night before. The Lenogue plant made mifepristone, one of two ingredients in the increasingly popular abortion pill. God's Gift Church, the largest and most influential anti-abortion entity in the new state, denied involvement through Kingston Avery, its leader.

Annie found herself captivated by the series of events, from the secession that resulted in Westcarolina's independence, to the midnight bombing of the abortion pill facility, and the politically savvy pastor leading the mega-church.

In Texas, she'd uncovered a large, dangerous nest of secessionists that had gone to ground in sparsely settled West Texas. The Nation of Texas was biding its time while it planned more violent acts to achieve its goal of Texas secession.

Annie considered herself somewhat of an expert on secession and wondered if the *Charlotte Press* might be interested in hiring her to investigate Westcarolina. She remembered that one of her former supervisors, Amanda Weeks, worked there in a high-level job. Managing editor? She thought so. Amanda had been a tremendous supporter of her work at the *Houston Times*.

The Charlotte newspaper had an excellent reputation for in-depth and investigative stories, though, like most papers, the financial problems of the industry had weakened it. She knew people considered Charlotte a mecca for growth and a nice place to live. Plus, it would be closer to her beloved alma mater in Chapel Hill and would enable her to ski and hike in Westcarolina.

She'd call Amanda later in the morning when her former boss at the *Houston Times* would likely be at the newspaper offices.

CHAPTER 4

Amanda drank two cups of coffee, preparing for two long editors' meetings at the *Charlotte Press*. At 8:30, her office phone rang. Like most mothers, she immediately panicked, worrying that something had happened to one of her children, though she'd taken them to school an hour previously. She breathed a sigh of relief when she immediately recognized the voice.

"Hi, Amanda. This is Annie Price, formerly of the *Houston Times*."

"Of course, Annie. How are you feeling?" Amanda felt guilty that she hadn't seen Annie for nearly a year.

"Great, although it's taken longer than I thought to heal."

"I've meant to call and check up on you sooner, but this job as managing editor came up and we had to move pretty quickly," Amanda said.

"How do you like Charlotte?"

"We love it. It's a great place for families and we've enjoyed exploring a new state. It's very different from Houston, with less traffic, pollution and an easier place to live."

"How are James and the kids?"

"Wonderful. James got a great job at one of the hedge funds, and Carolyn and Cameron like their new schools." Amanda looked at her watch. "What can I do for you, Annie?"

"I've followed the latest stories about last night's bombing, the new state, and the minister of the mega-church. As you may remember, secession is a special interest of mine. I'm wondering if there are any job possibilities."

"Actually, we're scouting for an investigative reporter to cover the new state and its strange new world. Right now, there's only one reporter assigned to it. You'd be perfect."

"Thank you, Amanda. How should I apply?"

"Why don't you leave it to me to take the temperature of the other editors? Then we can talk again. I've got the morning meeting that will morph into a planning meeting, so I might be able to broach your name today. I'll call you later."

"Wonderful, Amanda. I'll look forward to your call."

Amanda hung up the phone, feeling more optimistic than she had for several weeks. In her opinion, the paper hadn't done justice to the establishment of the new state. Reporters had covered each step dutifully without breaking any significant stories. There were excuses; a staff that layoffs and other departures had hollowed out, and the publisher's refusal to believe the state legislature would approve the secession.

Amanda remained in the top editor's office after the regular morning meeting for a discussion on the bombing and Westcarolina concerns. She was curious to see what would happen. Because of its institutional pride, she'd bet that the editors wouldn't publicly admit that they'd largely failed in their coverage.

The session took place in the office of Frank Billings, the paper's top editor; and included Amanda; Phil Perdue, the investigative editor; and Jim Markham, the Press's lone investigative reporter. Scheduling the meeting in the imposing glass office, with its conference table, maps and Frank's large, cluttered desk, underlined its importance. The news staff, which had always tried to decipher the tea leaves by looking through the glass, knew not to disturb any of the journalists.

An administrative assistant had supplied doughnuts and a pot of coffee. The participants filled their cups, but at first left the pastries on the table. As the meeting progressed, the sweets disappeared.

Amanda noticed that Phil took two, a plain one and one with nauseous-looking pink icing and multi-colored sprinkles. He was probably nervous. Why did the admin buy those awful-looking doughnuts that kids would love, but probably not adults? She supposed the store had run out of the plain variety.

"Who's taking responsibility for the bombing?" Frank asked. The top editor was a tall, thin, balding man who'd been the newsroom's chief leader for over ten years. He'd led the staff on projects that had won substantial awards. His quick mind bored rapidly into the heart of stories. Frank had come from the *Detroit Free Press*, when it became apparent that the city was falling apart. His wife was from Mississippi and was much happier when they returned to the South. They'd become big boosters of Charlotte.

"A group called Righteous Action," Phil said. "My best guess is that it's part of the Westcarolina leadership, but God's Gift Church's top dogs have denied it."

He'd been with the paper for eight years and had worked his way from reporter to investigative editor through his undisputed successes and unrelenting curiosity. He had the reputation of being a tough boss, but an unexpectedly kind man. Phil had unruly black hair that fell over his forehead, and a stocky build. He was from Massachusetts and was plain-spoken to a fault. Part of the newspaper's strength was hiring from multiple colleges, newspapers and different parts of the country, which contributed to a healthy diversity of opinion.

"Oh, those crazy people," Frank said.

"There's a method to their craziness," Phil said. "Look at what they likely did. They destroyed a factory that made hundreds of thousands of a key abortion pill ingredient each year. They didn't waste their time and energy bombing clinics."

Two inexperienced reporters, who comprised the slender weekend staff, had done a medium-sized story for page one. It focused on the Lenogue bombing, an explanation of the company's abortion drug and the death of its two night security guards. Tomorrow's paper would be an all-out effort of reporting in greater depth on the bombing, more background on the unprecedented secession, and the state's new leaders, Amanda knew.

She thought that Jim, the redheaded investigative reporter, probably felt the worst of anyone in the room. He'd tried to emphasize to his editors that the split of the western side of North Carolina from the rest of the state was imminent. Even more newsworthy, that its leaders probably would be the popular pastor of God's Gift Church and his second-in-command.

But like most reporters at the paper, Jim kept getting pulled away to cover unrelated stories. In recent weeks, he'd written about a recalcitrant school board, a grisly murder, and a big fire in a posh area of town.

Jim had come to the paper right out of North Carolina State University 15 years ago, and loved his work, but Amanda feared he was tiring of the constant upheavals in the office. His easygoing manner hid an intensely competitive brand of investigative reporting, but because he seemed so laid-back, people underestimated him.

"What exactly does King Avery want?" Frank asked.

"He wants a state where his church can impose its Draconian views," Phil said. "He wants to emphasize evangelical Christian values and to hell with the rest of the churches or people who don't go to church."

Frank's office had a large map of the Carolinas hanging on the wall, and Phil walked towards it. He used a pointer to show the counties west of Interstate 77 that'd seceded. He mentioned Westcarolina would take in 28 counties of lightly populated mountainous land, an area that the Press rarely wrote about because of its shrinking resources.

"Those areas—except for Asheville—are conservative, predominantly white populations that would be susceptible to the philosophy of God's Gift," Phil said.

"Why is Gastonia proposed as the capital?" Frank asked.

"Gastonia has everything they want—a sympathetic court system, conservative politicians and plenty of wealthy, influential people in the nearby Charlotte area. Gastonia church members give at least their share of money to Westcarolina's cause. The city is regarded as a bastion of God's Gift in an unpretentious county," Phil said.

"The new state wouldn't include Charlotte, right?" Amanda asked.

"Not formally," he said. "But most of their business interests and many church locations are here, so I expect we'll continue to see Charlotte as the unofficial epicenter of God's Gift and the financial underpinning of Westcarolina. As our paper is the largest in North Carolina and adjacent to Westcarolina, we have a special responsibility to cover it."

Frank began coordinating the special coverage for the next day. He ordered Jim to take the lead.

"You can bring in as many reporters from the news operation as you need," he said to Amanda.

"This is unprecedented. We need to find out who benefits, besides King Avery and his ultra-conservative church. And we need to start investigating how the church is going to use its new power and money."

"The best reporter to cover this new state is in Texas," Amanda said. "As you may recall, Annie Price won a Pulitzer a couple of years ago for her work, exposing corruption and violence within the secession movement there. She's an excellent journalist who doesn't quit on a big story. I have worked with Annie, and I think she'd be a wonderful partner for Jim."

"I agree," Jim said.

"That's a great idea," Phil said. "Can we squeeze money out of the budget to hire her, Frank?"

"Yes, we can, to get Annie," Frank said. "What's she doing these days?"

"Freelancing," Amanda said. "You know she was shot. She investigated that corrupt adoption center in the Hill Country of Texas. Annie took a leave of absence from the newspaper to heal, and decided not to go back when it changed the print product."

Amanda told Frank that she'd gotten a call from Annie early that morning after the reporter read about the bombing. She wanted to know if the top editors had a vacancy to cover the new state.

"Call her back immediately and tell her we're highly interested in speaking with her," Frank said.

CHAPTER 5

LEGISLATURE TENTATIVELY APPROVES NEW LEADERS OF WESTCAROLINA

By Jim Markham

The N.C. Legislature, which recently approved splitting North Carolina into two states, formally named two evangelical ministers as governor and lieutenant governor of the newly christened Westcarolina. Some of its functions will initially remain under North Carolina's control.

The action came six months after the outgoing president signed off on the creation of Westcarolina. As required, the state legislature and Congress endorsed the change.

The new state would include most of the N.C. territory west of Interstate 77 beyond Charlotte. It takes in Asheville, smaller towns and cities, mountainous areas and federal lands, such as the Great Smoky Mountains National Park. It encompasses 28 counties of about two million people in some of the most scenic land in North Carolina.

The recommendation to secede was highly controversial and came after repeated lobbying efforts from leaders of the powerful Charlotte-based God's Gift Church.

The legislature named Kingston Avery, 41, God's Gift pastor and executive director, as the first governor of the new state. Avery, with the agreement of the state legislature, named Henry Fullspear, 56, as lieutenant governor, making him Westcarolina's second-in-command. Both men will have to run for election in two years. Their appointments were no surprise—Avery had been all but anointed by influential national Republicans. The minister, who has had multiple congregations in Charlotte for ten years, has been a rising star in the evangelical world for most of that time. He has begun to establish outposts in Westcarolina. His God's Gift Church is believed to be the richest in the Carolinas.

Avery expressed gratitude that the state legislature and Congress had enough faith in their ministry to appoint them as the first leaders of Westcarolina.

"We don't take that responsibility lightly. I grew up in the mountains and always dreamed of starting a ministry there. The beautiful area will make up the first Christian state in our great United States. God bless America for making it happen."

Both Avery and legislative leaders cited what one called the biggest political advantage of the new state.

Westcarolina will get two new U.S. senators and at least two members of Congress, depending on redistricting. Presumably, given the region's strongly conservative bent, those politicians are more than likely to be Republicans, they said.

Because of that presumed benefit, the state legislature is more than willing to let Westcarolina go its own way on some matters.

The new state would still use some N.C. services, such as the highway patrol, social services and the motor vehicles division under contracts to be negotiated. After Westcarolina starts collecting taxes, probably within a year or two, it could still contract with North Carolina for those services or provide them on their own.

"We are happy to keep a relationship with the state of North Carolina while we figure out what Westcarolina can take on immediately," Avery said.

The new state, Avery and the God's Gift ministry are the subjects of several lawsuits, including a major effort to stop it by the American Civil Liberties Union.

Westcarolina will forbid the establishment of any abortion businesses, among other policies, Avery has said. Right now, it has several clinics in Asheville and Gastonia. Their operators said the businesses are shutting down.

Avery has refused to specify other changes he plans, which are thought to be substantial.

Federal sources have said privately they are examining whether Avery and his God's Gift ministry, which has a large contingent of anti-abortionists, bear any responsibility for last week's bombing. The action destroyed the Lenogue factory near Gastonia, which made one of the two ingredients in the abortion pill. The early morning bombing killed two security guards.

Avery has denied involvement in the bombing, though two activists being investigated in the explosion allegedly were once part of the ministry's now-defunct Righteous Action committee.

State and federal officials have declined to identify suspects, emphasizing that it is early in the investigation.

Lenogue officials said they won't rebuild in Gastonia.

"The poisonous atmosphere nurtured by God's Gift ministry and the new Westcarolina state it leads make it difficult, if not impossible, to operate there," Lenogue President Geoffrey Graham said.

Changes in borders have happened before in North Carolina. In 1712, the original colony of Carolina split into North Carolina and South Carolina because of the desire of England's financial backers to govern two smaller territories. South Carolina became a royal colony in 1719. North Carolina became a royal colony in 1729 and the king's officials appointed provincial governors. Government became more consistent, historians have said.

There have been no other comparable actions in modern times, though several states, including Alaska, Texas and California, have active secession movements.

(This is a developing story.)

CHAPTER 6

"How would you like to come to Charlotte and work for the *Press*?" Amanda asked on her cellphone. "I floated your name, and the upper-level editors quickly agreed you'd be the best person to cover Westcarolina."

Annie, pleased but wary, asked some pertinent questions before committing to a visit. If the paper didn't seem like a good fit, it would be pointless to waste both Amanda's time and hers.

"Would I have help covering the new state?"

"Yes, there's one other reporter who is assigned to it full time and others who can lend their skills, if needed," Amanda said. "As you know, most newspapers are more thinly staffed these days than they should be."

"Would I be doing investigative reporting in this position?" Annie found it fascinating to explore and uncover instances of wrongdoing or mismanagement.

"Initially, it would be wall-to-wall coverage of the creation of a new state," Amanda said. "But I hope you and our other enterprise reporter would use all your skills to do that. When things settle down in Westcarolina, you could certainly do other investigative stories."

"I'm game to come to Charlotte for an interview. We can check each other out," she said, easing her long legs off the countertop stool. She was antsy and needed to move around, so she walked around her kitchen. She stooped to pet the cats, who were both rubbing against her legs.

Amanda said she would set up meetings with the newspaper's investigative editor, reporter, the executive editor, the publisher, and a few others.

"That would be great," Annie said, impressed that the paper's hiring process was so thorough.

After the phone call ended, she pulled on some shorts (Houston in January was usually still shorts weather) and an oversized T-shirt embossed with the Texas flag. The casual outfit hid her slender figure but showcased her shapely legs. Annie was six feet tall, which she mostly found gave her an advantage over less imposing women. Men took her more seriously than petite reporters. Looking into the mirror, she twisted her thick black hair into a messy bun and applied sunscreen to her face, especially around her green eyes.

She tied on her size 10 sneakers and opened the door. Despite the winter morning, a blast of warm air hit her. Houston rarely registered huge temperature differences in the seasons. A January day was often warm, while a July day might hover around 100 degrees. It was just a question of how hot.

But it was the humidity that often drove people inside, especially workers, to the downtown tunnels that connected many of the larger buildings. Annie often had hurried through the maze of tunnels at work to grab a salad or a sandwich and return to the newspaper's frigid air conditioning. She accepted it as the cost of living in a vibrant city.

She'd seen the Houston region grow to six million people, with the attendant traffic and other problems. She'd looked up Charlotte quickly after Amanda's call and found that it had a metro area of 2.7 million, probably enough to make it interesting but likely with fewer of Houston's urban problems.

As she ran, she thought about the Westcarolina job, growing more excited by the moment. Her upper body had suffered the most injuries, and she was slowly regaining her previous stamina. By the time she'd run for a half-hour and had slowed down to cool off, rounding the corner of her treelined street, she'd decided. She'd go full throttle during the interviews and see how it worked out.

A week later, she flew to Charlotte, marveling at the size of the airport. In its large atrium, she enjoyed seeing the airport's iconic white rocking chairs and a young man playing a grand piano. The reason for the crowded concourses was that it was a hub airport. She thought that having hub status would give her an advantage for booking a nonstop flight to Houston or any other place.

She had dressed conservatively, in black pants, a silky white blouse, and a camel-colored blazer. Her hands were cold as she though of the job interviews ahead. However, she knew she was good at interviews because she had a career of experience interviewing others and skill at quick thinking. Amanda had implied that she was the *Press's* first and only contender.

Annie was pleased to find Amanda waiting for her in the baggage claim area. Dressed professionally in a black skirt and red blazer, the petite brunette welcomed Annie warmly. Annie really admired Amanda. The managing editor had grown up poor in one of the small refinery towns near Houston and had gone to the University of Texas on several scholarships. She'd joined the *Houston Times* as one of its youngest reporters and had advanced quickly. Annie especially liked her because she didn't have the tendency of some executive women to shut other women out. She had mentored more than a few young women on the paper.

Amanda took her to the *Press's* uptown building, a 1960s behemoth in what Annie knew was the Brutalist style of architecture. It was chunky and rectangular with narrow, slitted windows. She was relieved that the newspaper still had substantial headquarters in the center city. Many newspapers had sold their valuable center city land, and some had no headquarters at all, with staff members all working from home. She would hate to lose the camaraderie of a traditional newsroom.

Along the way, Annie enjoyed the sights of uptown (she was to learn that Charlotteans preferred the name uptown to downtown), its impressive skyscrapers set against a verdant mix of trees and large planters full of winter flowers. In the summer, Amanda told her, the planters were a riot of color with warm-weather growth. Annie learned that at night, the tops of the tallest skyscrapers were lit up for various causes and reasons, including blue before Carolina Panthers games and pink during breast cancer month. The football stadium and almost-new baseball complex, within walking distance of the newspaper office, drew regional crowds. It all looked festive and lively.

The uptown area also looked remarkably clean, and there were plenty of condos and apartment buildings hinting at vigorous city life. Several interesting-looking museums dotted lower Tryon, uptown's main street. Most people on the street wore nice work clothes and walked briskly with obvious purpose. She also noticed that there were some homeless people and wondered if Charlotte was working on solutions to the perpetual issue. Several men who appeared poor, but probably weren't homeless, were playing in an amateur band on a street corner.

It was so different from Houston's downtown, which so often felt steamy and full of strangers who thought nothing of jostling you if you got in their way. Houston had plenty of panhandlers, and sometimes they were downright threatening. It had fewer uptown apartments where young people would want to live. A few years ago, developers had bought and torn down the newspaper headquarters' signature white building. The *Times* had moved to a multi-story, modern-looking building near a major freeway, once owned by its now-defunct competitor. It was beautifully decorated inside, but it wasn't the same as being downtown.

Would it be nicer to live in a scrubbed-looking smaller place, or just stifling? It was the question that kept bothering her. If she got the job, time would tell, she thought. She remembered that Charlotte in her Chapel Hill days looked small when she drove by it on the highway, though it was regarded as a regional center at least 20 years ago.

The first level of the *Press* building was spacious and somewhat dim, with a security guard and a versatile office for public inquiries. Amanda took her to the escalators in the atrium of the building and they got on the one going up. The managing editor waved and chatted briefly with people as they went by on the escalator. Annie thought it was strange to have escalators in a newspaper building, but a rather charming way to communicate. She mentioned it to Amanda.

"Well, unfortunately, they break down a lot," said Amanda, laughing. "I think the elevators get a lot of use."

The large L-shaped newsroom on the fourth floor had a quiet atmosphere, with reporters and editors absorbed in their work. Annie found it impressive that it was just before 10 a.m. and the denizens of the newsroom seemed so busy. Sometimes in Houston, it was after 11 a.m. before the newsroom folks really got going and started making calls. The top brass had been liberal about start times because often the morning commute for journalists was exceptionally long. There had been so many people in the Houston newsroom and downtown news bureaus like the police station (always known as the cop shop) that it was hard to keep track of them. She and Amanda headed toward the managing editor's office, where about a dozen staffers were gathering for the morning meeting that critiqued the day's paper and set the agenda for the next day.

"Hey, everyone," Amanda said. "We have a visitor today. Meet Annie Price. She's looking at some jobs on the paper."

She was to learn that the editors usually introduced visitors that way, declining to be specific about exactly why they were there. Of course, the newsroom grapevine knew all about Annie and that she was applying for the plum job of an investigative reporter.

Amanda complimented the reporters who had worked on the Westcarolina package in that day's paper.

"Great reporting," she told the investigative editor. "Let's keep the momentum going."

Phil and the other editors quickly planned follow-ups for the next week, including a comprehensive profile of the evangelical minister and how he might lead the state.

"I'm sure many Westcarolina residents are very unhappy that the legislature has sold them down the river for two new conservative senators," Amanda said.

"King had better stop talking about Westcarolina being the first Christian state," Phil added. "Doesn't he know that the Constitution guarantees separation of church and state? When we schedule an interview with him, we should question him closely about that. Maybe he'll stop saying it, at least."

Amanda concluded the morning meeting faster than was usually the case in Charlotte, signaling to Annie to wait in the conference room while she gathered some other editors.

Annie prepared to be grilled.

CHAPTER 7

Annie sat listening quietly while Amanda outlined the agenda for the rest of her two-day visit. The newspaper had arranged for her to stay at a nice uptown hotel, but the night wasn't exactly restful. She'd tossed and turned until the early morning hours, thinking about the events of the day.

She'd interviewed with a variety of editors yesterday, would talk to a few more today, and thought she'd done well. She fielded all their questions easily, and she sensed they liked her. They impressed her as well, and that they would hire an investigative reporter at the top of their salary scale meant something.

Today, and most crucial, was her meeting with Fordham Carter III, the newspaper's longtime publisher. Most of the newsroom editors seemed to fear and despise him, and they had good reason to do so. She'd heard that Carter had a significantly more conservative stance compared to the mostly progressive staff. Occasionally, he would return editorials and cartoons for revision because he thought they were too liberal.

Amanda kept her company on the short escalator ride down to the third floor, where the newspaper administrators had glass offices. Annie noted that the largest office unsurprisingly belonged to Carter. His secretary waved her into the reception area. Carter came out of his office quickly and shook her hand politely. They entered his spacious office, and he gestured for her to sit in the chair opposite his grand mahogany desk.

"So, this is the young lady who's supposed to be the expert on separatist movements," Carter said in a voice just short of mocking. Great way to start the meeting, she thought.

The publisher was about five feet six, she guessed, in his late 50s, with thinning blond hair and pale gray eyes. She wondered if he would hold her six-foot height against her, as some insecure shorter men had done in her past. Others seemed impressed by it, which pleased her. However, she wished that her commanding height would just be a non-issue.

"I covered the secessionist movement in Texas and a separatist movement in the state's Hill Country. The secessionists wanted to create a new country out of Texas, while the separatists wanted to carve out a region to focus on their German heritage.

"The secessionists are still active, particularly in West Texas, but the German Texans gave up after a key leader was murdered."

"I'll bet that was a strange time," Carter said. "It's commendable that you covered both of them at once."

Annie nodded and smiled briefly. She appreciated the kind comments and the fact that he'd apparently researched her history. Maybe he wasn't so bad after all.

"That was before the *Houston Times* went from a primarily print newspaper to a bigger website and smaller print product. I left the paper about a year ago when I got shot on the job."

"I heard about what happened with that corrupt adoption agency and the crazy South American woman who shot you," Carter said. "Did they ever find her?"

"No, and I don't expect they ever will," Annie said. She felt impressed that he'd researched another one of her top projects, although the shocking news of her shooting had spread throughout the journalism world.

She moved quickly to start a discussion of the new state, eager to hear his views.

Carter said that while his staff was suspicious of Westcarolina, he was reserving judgment.

"Our staff members, like most newspaper people, are a godless bunch," he said. "King Avery wants to make something good out of Westcarolina, and the least we can do is to keep an open mind."

Annie thought it was obvious he wasn't keeping an open mind. She also disliked the fact that he had called newspaper people "godless." She knew plenty of journalists who were religious, and he ought to know that, too. Most publishers were reasonably tolerant, especially about the religious preferences of their staff. So what if some reporters and editors weren't believers? That wasn't exactly a prerequisite for working for a newspaper. In fact, turning down job applicants because of religion—or lack of it— was illegal.

"How do you know Kingston Avery?" she asked.

"We have homes in the same neighborhood of Blowing Rock," Carter said. She thought he must be wealthy to have a vacation home in the same neighborhood as the pastor. Wonder if he agreed with the church's evangelical philosophy and beliefs?

"Have you known him for a long time?"

"Probably about five years," Carter said. "That's when he finished his house up on the mountain. It's a showplace."

"What's he like?"

"He's a wonderful person, unassuming, friendly, and down-to-earth. I knew his grandfather before the old man passed, and the Rev. Avery was a real fire-and-brimstone guy. There were rumors that he was a snake handler, but I don't think people outside his church knew for sure.

"King is more mainstream," Carter said with a smile. "He's passionate about his work and beloved by the thousands of people in his congregation."

"Are you one of them?"

"No, I don't belong to any church," Carter said. "I drop in on a few now and then."

Annie decided it was time to tackle other subjects. She'd read plenty about the Charlotte paper and its prospects, but she wanted to know what the publisher thought. She'd ask him softball questions.

"How do you think the newspaper is doing? Is advertising holding up?"

"It's certainly not what it was five years ago," Carter said. "But if Charlotte keeps growing the way it is, we'll likely survive. That doesn't mean we wouldn't consider a change in ownership if the family wants to sell. The family gets offers and always considers them, especially lately, as the older generation wants to retire from the board.

"I wouldn't be surprised if a sale happens in the next year or two," Carter added.

This was worrisome, given that sales of newspaper businesses in recent years were to mediocre chains or wealthy but unpredictable entrepreneurs. Annie wondered if the newspaper's stability was something she ought to worry about. Usually, a sale brought more bad news than good.

"Do you see the newspaper going digital only?"

"We'll have to see where we are in a couple of years. We're fortunate that we've kept our staffing at a moderate level, but this Westcarolina business will ratchet up our needs.

"You've come here to interview at the right time, young lady," Carter said with a smile.

Annie hated it when men called her young lady. For one thing, she wasn't young. For another, it sounded so patronizing. But she certainly would not voice any objections during a crucial job interview.

"What about your circulation? Is it holding its own?" she asked, another simple question she thought publishers like to talk about. She knew the answer to most of these questions, having researched the paper thoroughly before making the trip.

Well, it certainly isn't gaining," he answered. "There's too much competition–Charlotte-based websites like *Axios* and the *Charlotte Ledger.* There's lots of TV news, big national newspapers that circulate here, and local radio stations that have expanded their capabilities.

"I would say that my biggest worry is that we might become less relevant, easier to do without. That's why we need to offer our readers something better."

He seemed to remember that he was talking to a reporter–and a bold one, at that.

"Ms. Price, I'm supposed to be asking the questions and you're to answer them," Carter said with an air of irritation.

"I'm sorry, Mr. Carter. It's useful to know what news executives think about the newspaper and King Avery, the leader of a brand-new state. Also, I'm justifiably concerned about the financial state of the paper, since I worked for one that had to reduce its scope considerably."

Carter nodded. She'd been worried but could see that her answer satisfied him.

"Well, I'm officially neutral, but I can see certain advantages in the new state," he said. "People would be better off if they gave up booze and cigarettes. I don't drink or smoke and I'm proud of it. If Westcarolina refuses to sell those dangerous products, more power to King."

Wow, she thought, he's kind of puritanical. Just hope he realizes that most people aren't. Most newsroom staffs drank plenty of alcohol, though smoking was much less prevalent than when Annie started working in journalism. Companies had banned smoking in newsrooms and entire buildings for years, and sometimes even the surrounding outdoor property. Annie, who was slightly asthmatic, had applauded each change.

Someone knocked on Carter's door. It was Amanda, who stuck her head in.

"We appreciate your taking the time to interview Annie," she said. "We promised we wouldn't take up your entire day, so we'll leave you to the rest of your schedule."

"No problem," Carter said. "It's obvious that she's a smart girl."

Annie winced when Carter called her a girl but kept smiling. That was another thing she detested, but obviously, she wouldn't confront him. She was used to restraining herself around older, less evolved men, biting her tongue.

Since Carter was Annie's last interview of the day, Amanda dropped her off at the hotel the newspaper had arranged.

"How did it go with Carter?"

"Interesting man. Not sure he liked me. I probably asked too many questions."

"You'd be surprised," said Amanda. "He likes people who stand up in tough interviews. He hates people who kowtow to him."

The next day, Annie got a job offer. It was generous and gave her free rein to investigate Westcarolina. She accepted.

CHAPTER 8

For the next two weeks, Annie focused on the move to Charlotte. She quickly sold her small Craftsman-style house in The Heights, a trendy part of Houston, happy that it garnered much more money than she'd paid for it. She thinned out her possessions and arranged for movers. *The Press* would give her temporary lodging and other benefits. Meanwhile, she had a couple of weeks left to stay in her beloved house.

How emotional she felt surprised her. The longtime friends she'd worked with at the Houston newspaper gave her a big party, renting La Carafe, her favorite downtown bar. It was a historic brick building located a few blocks from the former newspaper offices. The venerable place drew about 40 of her friends and the party lasted until the early hours of the morning. There was great vintage music and even some late-night dancing. Her longtime colleagues presented her with a pair of hiking boots she could wear in the Westcarolina mountains.

She regaled them with tales of the new state and its likely restrictions, such as banning tobacco and alcohol sales.

"You better start practicing giving up your daily glass of chardonnay," Travis Dunbar, her favorite reporter, said. "And how about your weekend partying? Not acceptable."

"I think anything that might be fun is banned," Annie said with a smile. "Travis, that would include your twice-a-week poker game."

Would she have as much fun and as many friends at the new paper? She doubted it, because she was older and more serious than in her early days at the Houston Times. Her friends had graduated from giving late-night apartment parties to getting married, having children and mostly staying home on weekends.

Now came a task she'd been dreading. For the last year, Annie had toggled between two out-of-town boyfriends. Tom Marr was a former gubernatorial candidate and ex-secessionist she'd first written about, then dated, after he'd left the secessionist movement, and she'd stopped covering him. Her other romantic interest was Jake Satterfield, a powerful lawyer and former legislator living in Austin she'd first met through the paper's coverage. She needed to let both know she was about to move.

Since Tom was 600 miles away and Jake about 170, she'd been able to avoid the subject successfully for two weeks. Whenever he didn't have his kids for the weekend, she saw Jake every couple of weeks, but it was harder for Tom to travel so far from West Texas. She didn't see Tom often, but they talked on the phone frequently. She hadn't mentioned the Charlotte offer. It was time—probably way past time.

She called Tom at his mammoth cattle ranch. He sounded crushed at her imminent departure. She felt guilty that she soon would be even farther away. She nervously drummed her fingers on her countertop and tried to think of ways to be positive.

"Betsy will be so disappointed," he said. "You know you're very important in her life."

Betsy was Tom's eighteen-year-old daughter who'd become infatuated with a guitar player she'd met at a concert in El Paso when she was sixteen. The musician had persuaded her to run away to Houston with him. When Annie found Betsy, the teen was working in a topless bar and supporting the abusive man she was living with. Annie helped her to get away from the job and the bad boyfriend and brokered a reunion with her father. Betsy returned to the ranch and went back to high school.

"Betsy's about to go off to the University of Texas," Annie said. "She knows I love her, and I'll try to visit her often. But she'll have plenty to do in Austin, and I doubt if she'll miss either of us much."

"I always thought we'd get married," he said with regret. "You know you're the perfect woman for me."

"Tom, we've discussed that," she said in a small, sad voice. "You can't leave your ranch and there are no real professional jobs for me in West Texas. This job in Charlotte is a great opportunity and I can't afford to pass it up. For one thing, I haven't worked for a while, and I need the salary."

She felt terrible, springing the move on him so near the time of her departure. She'd been dreading it so much.

He was quiet for a moment, then gave her an uncharacteristic piece of advice.

"Annie, you're always so busy chasing stories you're not living the good life you could have," he said. "I think getting shot made you temporarily lose your incredible work ethic, but it seems to be back. Do you really want to grow old with just a pile of stories as your legacy? Marry me, have a kid or two and slow down on your work. You'll be happier in the long run."

"I think that's unfair, Tom. There's nothing wrong with being serious about your work. Besides, I think I've already missed the boat on having a child. Maybe you and I can synchronize our work situations in a year or two. But you should continue to date. You know we've never been exclusive."

"That's because of that shyster lawyer in Austin," he said. "You're wasting your time with him."

"Oh, Tom. Let's not argue about this tonight, please."

She knew that her double love life was a sore point with both men, who couldn't stand each other anyway because of skirmishes in the secessionist movement. Jake had supported the secessionists until he became disenchanted with their extreme program years ago. Tom, who'd run for governor on a secessionist platform, took longer to disavow the movement. He'd quit when he found violent and corrupt supporters behind its idealistic façade.

"'Okay, darlin.' I'd like to visit you often. Charlotte's only a few hours away."

"Sure, Tom. You know I'd look forward to visits from you."

The tug of her career had always been something that kept them from marrying. Another reason was because she hadn't been able to give up Jake Satterfield.

Tom resembled a Viking, she'd always thought. With his striking appearance, standing at 6 feet, 5 inches with grayish-blonde hair and a rancher's tan, he undeniably adored her. A widower, he was a wonderful guy, devoted to Betsy and kind and fair to the people who worked for him. He also had a wry, self-effacing sense of humor that appealed to Annie. He was the consummate West Texan, with a down-home drawl and courtly manners with women.

Jake was just a little taller than her six feet, with dark brown hair and an appealing grin he flashed often. Before he and his wife Jeannie separated six years ago, Annie had dated Jake, but ended the relationship when his estranged wife unexpectedly became pregnant with their son. He conceded that he'd made a big mistake sleeping with Jeannie in a moment of weakness but couldn't abandon her while she was pregnant. He and Annie had started dating again a year ago when Jake's marriage broke up for good. Annie was afraid to commit herself fully to Jake because he was a workaholic and a flirt. Besides, he lived three hours away from Houston and was often inaccessible.

However, Jake was very sexy, with a fun-loving approach to life that she appreciated. But he'd broken her heart when he went back to his ex-wife. Could she fully trust him again?

She loved Jake and Tom both—in slightly different ways. Those feelings for two men were a predicament she'd never really faced. After a year of dating both, she still didn't know what to do. She had expected her love life to be more established by the time she turned 42.

"Can I come to Houston and see you before you leave?" Jake asked during their phone call. Of course, she answered.

He drove to Houston the next night, and they shared a long kiss at the door. He came inside and petted her cats while she poured him a large glass of red wine.

"I thought we'd get married when my divorce is final," he said. Her heart beat a little faster with those words.

"That sounds so romantic," she said with an ironic smile. "But I've got to take this job. I need to work again, and it'll be a wonderful challenge for me."

"But what about me?" he said with unusual passion. "You know I can't get along without you."

"Well, honey, you survived for four years without me," she said, trying to play it light.

"Yeah, well, I was miserable," he said. "You know I tried to renew my relationship with my wife for my kids' sake–while she was having an affair with my best friend."

"I realize that was very hard on you, but you made up for it by dating every eligible woman in Austin after you first separated from her," Annie said. She was kidding but knew that Jake had played the field assiduously before they started dating again. She also had heard that he still saw at least one woman in Austin–a TV reporter.

"Yeah, what about you and Mr. Hotshot Cowboy?" Jake said in an injured tone.

Oh no, not this again, she thought to herself.

"I wish you two would stop hating on each other, Jake. You know you and I haven't been exclusive."

"Baby, I might want to change that," he said. She thought he sounded serious, but she wasn't willing to have that conversation on the brink of leaving town.

"Dinner's almost ready. Let's finish up our drinks," she said. "I want this to be a pleasant evening." She'd made Chicken Kiev with mashed potatoes and Brussels sprouts and a lemon cake for dessert.

The evening that started with discord ended slowly and languorously in her bedroom.

The next morning, she tearfully kissed him goodbye. After he left–with promises to visit her soon in Charlotte–Annie cried. She was leaving two men who cared deeply about her for a new place where she knew no one. Was the move a mistake?

CHAPTER 9

Annie had been at the Charlotte Press for just a few days when Amanda and Phil called an important planning meeting with her and Jim.

She was getting to know Jim since they sat across from each other in a corner of the newsroom. Known as the investigative pod, it included the two of them, plus their editor, Phil.

Jim was red-haired with freckles and a tall, skinny build. Her new partner was a few years younger than Annie's 42, but she felt he was an equal in every way. He'd won many awards, especially when there were more staffers on the investigative team, and he'd had more time to work on longer stories. He was witty, smart and knew all the politics and quirks of the paper. Annie enjoyed being around him.

Phil looked the part of a newspaper editor, with rumpled clothes and a general air of disrepute that was deceptive. He was a strong investigative editor, and Annie found him to be sensitive to the human side of issues. He seemed very welcoming, and she thought he'd probably been desperate for more staffing to cover this enormous story.

She thought how lucky she was to have an editor and fellow reporter who shared her own ambitions and principles.

The two editors had arranged a lunch session to plan more coverage of the new state of Westcarolina. It would be a monumental task for the two reporters, though they'd get help from a few other staffers on breaking-news stories.

The editors and reporters munched on chicken salad sandwiches and giant chocolate chip cookies from a nearby deli while they exchanged ideas. The restaurant also sent iced tea with sugar, lemon, and mint, as befitting Charlotte's love of sweet tea.

"Annie, how do you think we should approach this?" Amanda asked. "I'm sure you learned a lot covering the secessionists in Texas."

Annie's Houston reporting for several years had centered on the secessionist movement as it eventually took over part of the western end of the state. Certain sparsely populated areas now had a reputation for danger that kept most tourists from visiting.

"I think the first thing we should do is to look for two families, one in favor of Westcarolina and one against it, and follow the state's activities through their views," Annie said. "Over the next year, we can see if their attitudes and lifestyles change.

"I can look for families with a couple of children each, one family living in Asheville and the other in the capital of Gastonia. Since Asheville is the most liberal area and Gastonia is the conservative capital, there would likely to be interesting differences."

"That's a good idea," Jim said. "Perhaps I can start interviewing some businesses in Asheville to find how much they're worried about this administration. The largest city will be most affected."

"That's going to be a major effort in itself," said Annie. "Might as well get started."

Amanda gave her blessing to the concept and said both reporters should start looking for their sources right away. She also assigned long-term coverage of the new governor, King Avery, to Annie and lieutenant governor Henry Fullspear to Jim.

"You both should work on the big issues that are likely to come up," Amanda said. "This first couple of years will be crucial. The legislature has said it will support Westcarolina's essential services like the highway patrol for two years—until the new state can set up its own tax collection system. Soon, Westcarolina will have to contract with North Carolina for some services. That should be very interesting."

Talk turned to King, his magnetic appeal to his growing flock and its importance to the evangelical movement.

"I've met him a few times and tried to investigate some of his excesses, like the 12-bedroom mansion in the mountains," Jim said. "I've heard that he has wild parties, but you have to be a big giver to get invited."

"Wild parties in what way?" Amanda asked with curiosity.

"Sex and drugs. I know that sounds hard to believe, but King apparently has a side that his Sunday sermons don't cover."

"He's a damn hypocrite," said Phil, who never minced words. "That certainly is something to look at, Annie. It's hard to visualize what a wild party in the God's Gift ministry would look like."

"I see plenty of avenues to investigate," Annie said. "I will set up a get-acquainted interview as soon as he'll see me." She was excited by all the possibilities and the enthusiasm of the editors. She loved starting a major story and plotting its course. Working with Jim and influential editors who understood its importance was a big plus. She felt flattered that they began consulting her before she really knew much about the big story.

The four journalists brainstormed for two hours and felt they had a good starting plan. They agreed to hold a major planning meeting every two weeks.

After work, Annie had an appointment with a real estate broker. She was living in a small corporate apartment in a high-end commercial area called SouthPark and was eager to get settled in a place of her own. Even her cats seemed restless.

The broker had recommended two neighborhoods near uptown that she thought would suit Annie. One, Dilworth, was more expensive than Plaza Midwood. Annie had made a considerable profit on her Houston house and was a big saver. But houses in Charlotte were more expensive than she'd thought. She felt she could afford a small house in Plaza Midwood. It was an older neighborhood with a trendy central street that included interesting restaurants and bars.

The area was home to many other *Press* staffers. It reminded her of the trendy neighborhood in Houston where she'd lived.

She was despairing over the high prices when the broker showed her a small frame cottage with wood floors, high ceilings and two bedrooms. The kitchen was tiny and needed updating, so it had sat on the market for a while.

Annie cooked little, so the small, outdated kitchen didn't bother her. She could renovate it as she saved more money. She presented an offer that was accepted by the following day. Annie realized that buying a house so soon yoked her to Charlotte and cut most of her ties to Houston, but she felt ready to make the change.

CHAPTER 10

Annie quickly found two couples she'd talk to on a continuing basis. Janet and James Pardel, in their early forties, lived in Asheville. Barbara and Bob Aydlette were in their mid-thirties and lived in Gastonia. As she'd told her editors, she wanted relationships with at least two couples who were strongly in favor or against the new state.

While the creation of the new state overjoyed the Aydlettes, the Pardels strongly disagreed with the concept of Westcarolina. The Pardels, a Black family with self-described progressive views, included two teenagers. The Aydlettes, who were white, and called themselves conservatives, were parents of a preschooler and a third grader. Seeing the new state through the couples' differing viewpoints would give a nuanced, close-up picture, Annie thought. Jim had contacted some business leaders he'd go to regularly. He and Annie also would talk to residents in other parts of the new state, by phone, email or in person, when they could break away from daily news stories.

One morning, soon after talking with her couples over the phone, Annie traveled to Asheville to meet with the Pardels. It was her first glimpse of the mountain city, about three hours from Charlotte. Its distinctive downtown, featuring several attractive squares and historic buildings, left a favorable impression on Annie. She knew that famed author Thomas Wolfe grew up there and resolved to make time to visit his house, which was open to the public. She also vowed to return another time to see the gigantic Biltmore Estate, the largest privately owned home in the United States. The Biltmore especially had other attractions, such as gorgeous flower gardens and its own winery and wine-tasting rooms.

The beautiful city was mostly cool in the summer, but had some snow and ice in the winter, which made would-be residents think twice before moving there. Annie liked the hills and nearby mountains around the city. If she'd had a choice, she'd consider living in Asheville rather than Charlotte, because of Asheville's beauty and progressive vibe. But she knew she'd have to stay in Charlotte where the excellent job was, and she'd eventually find people she liked, inside and outside the paper. Besides, Charlotte was a larger and more diverse city with many more cultural and leisure attractions to be explored.

Annie had timed her visit with the Pardels on Saturday when both Janet and James were available. Janet, a lawyer with the American Civil Liberties Union, was tall and slender with a modest Afro. James, a high school teacher in the Asheville public schools, was balding and slightly overweight. He also was a leader in the civil rights movement there. She liked them immediately, and she was impressed that despite their busy jobs and family life, they spent time and energy trying to better their community. They'd come from Orlando, Fla. to escape the heat, the suffocating presence of Disney World and the conservative state politics. They loved the five years they'd spent in Asheville.

Janet and James had agreed to meet at one of their favorite downtown restaurants for brunch, the Early Girl Eatery. They all ordered one of the restaurant's signature offerings–chicken tenders and biscuits. They enjoyed their Southern-themed food as they talked.

"We both think the new state will be a disaster," Janet said. "Already we're hearing rumors of things that may change–and not for the better."

"Tell me more," Annie said.

"King Avery hates Asheville because it's tolerant of gays, Wiccans, atheists and other citizens that have every right to be different," Janet said. "His evangelical congregations aren't accepting of differences and people who don't go to God's Gift Church.

"I'm sure you know that with 500,000 people, the Asheville metro area is by far the largest in the new state," she noted. "Parts of its four counties are more open-minded than most of Westcarolina. Asheville alone has a population of 93,000 people, most of whom believe in letting people live their own lives. There are comparatively few Blacks here, but we've felt welcome and made a lot of friends."

James expressed concern that Asheville could face consequences for its liberal politics and inclusive attitudes that many practiced.

"In what ways would Asheville be punished?" Annie asked.

"Certain establishments, such as bars and tattoo studios, will probably face closure or significant modifications," he said. "But that may be just the beginning. I never thought I'd see a second Prohibition era, but that's what King Avery and his God's Gift Church seem to want."

"Other rumored proposals, such as banning tobacco products, would be patently illegal, plus deprive the new state of lots of tax revenue," Janet Pardel said. "I'm not a smoker. I worry about tobacco users who knowingly expose themselves to all kinds of cancer and heart problems. But again, God's Gift Church has set itself up as Big Brother, and that's just wrong."

Annie was thoughtful as she left the Pardels. Did they really have legitimate fears or were they just being paranoid? She'd ask King Avery about Asheville if she got to interview him anytime soon. So far, his staff was putting it off. She was going to have to be more insistent the next time she talked to them.

She thought that Gastonia, a satellite city of Charlotte with a population of 72,000, looked vastly different from Asheville. Compared to Charlotte, the city had a tired looking downtown, though it was called, rather grandly, the Gastonia Historic District. She knew that Gastonia once had been a thriving center for textile manufacturing and still had a heavily blue-collar population, characteristics that suited the demographics of God's Gift. She'd noted that Charlotte residents made fun of Gastonia, which she felt was unfair but was typical of bigger cities. Houstonians had always made fun of the adjacent city of Pasadena, which was rife with refineries and related businesses.

She'd arranged for a late afternoon meeting with her Gastonia couple, Barbara and Bob Aydlette, at one of the city's big attractions, Tony's Ice Cream parlor. The business made the ice cream next door in many flavors. The restaurant also drew a wide swath of area residents who enjoyed its sandwiches and other short orders. The Aydlettes welcomed her warmly—it was obvious they were proud of the local landmark and eager to talk about the new state.

Annie ordered a banana milk shake and started asking questions. Barbara, a petite blonde dressed casually in jeans, was a hospital nurse who worked three 12-hour shifts a week to have more time with her children. Bob, dark-haired and slim, was a firefighter. They were both enthusiastic about King Avery and had been members of the God's Gift Church in Gastonia for seven years. The church formed the crux of their social life, with its suppers and men's, women's and children's groups. The Aydlettes were lifelong residents of Gastonia, and all their extended family members lived there, too.

"Gastonia is just right for us," Barbara said. "Charlotte is too big, with too much bad traffic. But it has good theatre, parks, and excellent shopping. I wouldn't want to live there, though."

Annie was to find that such criticisms were common from residents of smaller towns. Even the legislature referred to Mecklenburg County, where Charlotte was located, as "the great state of Mecklenburg" and routinely stinted on its needs, including better roads.

Lately the Aydlettes had moved into one of God's Gift subdivisions—Annie had heard that new housing was one of King Avery's latest schemes to make money. They lived on Godly Circle in a three-bedroom, two-bath ranch house. There were rumors that the prices for the new homes were 30 percent higher than new ones of comparable size. God's Gift officials would probably skim that percentage off the top, theoretically, to support church programs. But Annie wondered if it instead was lining the pockets of King Avery.

"What are you looking forward to in the new state?" Annie said.

"Everything," Bob said promptly. "No abortion, no tobacco, no alcohol, no weird-looking people with terrible morals. Instead, our lives will center on God and his will."

"How can you be sure what that is?" Annie asked. She had already told them, in response to Barbara's question, that she wasn't a churchgoer.

"Whatever King Avery preaches for and against is how to have a godly life," Barbara said. "My goodness, Annie, you need to listen to him and get your head on straight. I don't want to see a nice person like you go to hell."

"Did you realize when you bought your new house that it was priced higher than the market to support King Avery's ministry?" Annie said.

"I haven't checked around much," Bob said. "But surely, being part of God's Gift ministry will increase its value."

"Are you surprised about the creation of the new state?"

"We definitely were surprised, but it was a pleasant surprise," Barbara said.

"It's like a dream come true."

After answering more questions, the Aydlettes said they needed to get home to relieve the babysitter, so they all said their goodbyes.

"Over the phone, I'd like to check in with you every few weeks to see how you're feeling about the latest news on Westcarolina," Annie said. "That okay?"

"Of course, honey," Barbara said. "In the meantime, if you want to go to church with us, please let me know."

CHAPTER 11

Just a day after meeting with the Aydlettes, King Avery summoned Annie to his Blowing Rock home. At least that's what it felt like to her.

She'd been asking for an interview since she started work at the *Press* two weeks previously, but the God's Gift staffers had put her off. She suspected that now, word had gotten back that she had interviewed the Aydlettes, who were church stalwarts. That likely paved the way.

She dressed carefully in her best work clothes—a black suit with a knee-length pencil skirt, a hot pink long-sleeved blouse and pearls. She put her hair up in a low bun.

The drive was a breeze, passing a couple of uneventful small towns until she neared Blowing Rock. Suddenly, she could see the tiers of misty mountains in the distance. She sighed with pleasure—how she'd missed this. She'd traveled around those mountains during her childhood, living in East Tennessee and southwest Virginia. In the middle of the day, the sun on the mountains created a spectacular sight.

She knew she was looking at the Blue Ridge Mountains. Their blue haze, a reflection of the blue-green fir and balsam forests that grew there, was distinctive. Leisurely drivers flocked to the gorgeous Blue Ridge Parkway in autumn to see red, yellow and orange fall colors. In the spring and summer, tourists could look forward to the healthy foliage sprinkled with wildflowers. Annie thought the mountains were equally beautiful when covered by snow, with just the tops of some trees sticking out.

She'd researched the mountains when she knew she was about to cover Westcarolina. The Blue Ridge Mountains were part of the Appalachian range that drew hikers and other tourists from Maine to Georgia. The long, arduous Appalachian Trail had daunted many hikers over the years but had given an immense sense of accomplishment to those who could complete its formidable length. Other parts of the Appalachians in Westcarolina included the Smoky Mountains and the Black Mountains. The Smoky Mountains were home to the popular national park. The Black Mountains near Asheville featured Mount Mitchell, the highest peak in the chain at nearly 7,000 feet.

Houston was flat as a board and had made her long for the mountains. But she loved Galveston Beach, about fifty miles away and the rugged, bare mountains of Big Bend National Park, 600 miles across Texas. Every state was wonderful, if you remained open to its brand of beauty, she reflected. She was lucky that she'd learned to love everywhere she'd lived. She felt sure it would be the same way with Charlotte. Journalists had to be endlessly flexible.

She drove through the resort town of Blowing Rock, with its main street and a few side streets of specialty shops, restaurants and a city park. She vaguely remembered Blowing Rock from visiting relatives in East Tennessee and driving through the town with her family. With her father at the wheel late at night smoking cigarettes, she often got carsick. The high, curvy roads made things worse. Now the roads were of much better quality. She hoped she could take time soon to explore the Blowing Rock area on her own. Today, she couldn't stop thinking about the interview that would take place in just a few minutes.

She reached King Avery's address, at the top of a nearby ridge, and had no trouble spotting the house. It was a spectacular example of a French chateau, featuring white columns across the front. She knocked on the door, which was answered by a housekeeper, who told her to take a seat. The spacious, paneled living room, with its soaring ceilings, contained luxurious, French furnishings and a floor-to-ceiling row of windows in the back that offered a panoramic view of the mountains. Outside, Annie could see a stone patio with the same stunning view. It had what looked like a fancy outdoor kitchen and patio and was large enough to accommodate medium-size events. Annie idly wondered if that was the area where King held the allegedly wild parties. She thought the preacher had hardly taken a vow of poverty.

A gorgeous woman walked through the large living room, stopped by Annie's chair, and introduced herself.

"Hello," she said, extending a well-manicured hand. "I'm Claire Avery. You must be the new reporter at the *Charlotte Press*."

"I'm Annie Price," Annie said, standing to shake her hand. "I'm here to meet your husband. Meeting you is an unanticipated bonus."

Claire smiled and sat on the sofa beside Annie's plush chair. Annie noticed she was medium tall, slender to the point of being skinny and had a cap of white-blonde hair combed in a punk style. Her hairstyle gave her an interesting look that hinted of hidden, perhaps rebellious, depths. Her beige pants and sweater suited her pale, flawless complexion. She appeared to be about 40. They chatted for a few minutes.

The appearance of a tall, blond man, dressed in form-fitting jeans and a plaid shirt, interrupted the conversation between Annie and Claire. He had a handsome face that hinted of friendliness. He moved with a quiet confidence Annie thought must result from the adoration of the thousands of church members. It had to be King Avery.

"Hello, Reverend Avery," she said, standing to shake his hand. Claire disappeared silently from the room.

"Please call me King. Everyone does."

He led her to his study. It was spacious and imposing, with an expensive beige sofa and a leather chair across from a clutter-free desk. Annie could see a large conference room through an open door behind the study. She chose the chair nearest his desk and got out her notebook and cellphone to record the interview. She noted photographs on the wall of King and a former U.S. president; with other preachers, such as Jerry Falwell Jr.; and what appeared to be ministers from King's churches. There were no personal family photos.

King sat down and studied her for a minute, which seemed odd. She smiled, and he continued to stare at her fixedly, not in a flirtatious way. She hoped she'd dressed conservatively enough, and her makeup hadn't smeared. There must be something strange about her, though, with his gaze still assessing her.

"You're pregnant," he said. "Congratulations."

Shock overwhelmed Annie. Not only was it presumptuous; it couldn't be right. She played it light.

"I'm an old lady of 42. Why would you think such a thing?"

"My grandmother was Irish and was what they call fey. I inherited her second sight, to some extent. It's not infallible, but it helps me with my ministry. You walked in, and I just knew. I could see you with a beautiful blond boy."

Annie felt rattled. She was thinking back and wondering if it might be true. She remembered the romantic evening with Jake just a few weeks ago. Annie hadn't used contraception, mainly because she'd gone off the pill. She'd had issues in the past that convinced her she was infertile.

"Anything else you need to know?" he said in a teasing voice.

She knew she had to start asking her questions immediately, or the interview would be wasted. She already had a lot of background on him, so she could move directly into Westcarolina questions.

"When did you get the idea for Westcarolina?" she said.

"I've always wanted a land where godly people put religion first. I became friends with the former president, and he wanted to help. When he filed his executive order at the end of his term of office designating 28 North Carolina counties as Westcarolina, my people were ecstatic. Of course, I've spent years of lobbying part-time for the change at the state and national level.

"We have a dozen churches in the Charlotte region, some of them in schools. I can preach to all members with today's technology. Now I can spread God's word throughout our new territory."

"The outlier in your new state is Asheville," Annie said. "How does a liberal city fit in with the more conservative areas?"

"Asheville will be an integral part of our ministry. I don't think it will take the area long to adjust to our ways."

"How will you accomplish that?"

"We're awfully persuasive," King said with a smile. "People usually like us when they find out more about us. We have a very high approval rating in our counties—almost 70 percent overall, and higher in some of the westernmost counties. People have been so welcoming that I could travel to a different county every night to speak and draw a large crowd. But that would take valuable time away from governing, so I can't do that. When we have an important message, we discuss it on the God's Gift TV station."

"What will be the biggest changes in Westcarolina?"

"We will not tolerate abortion businesses or sales of tobacco and likely will introduce substantial restrictions on alcohol," King said. "Other decisions are still on the table. Tobacco and abortions are among the greatest scourges of humanity."

Annie reminded him that growing certain varieties of tobacco, such as burley, had a long, storied history in western North Carolina.

"Tobacco kills 400,000 people a year," King said. "A godly state would do something about that."

"You said your God's Gift churches would be located across the new state, using a combination of public buildings and new construction, as in Charlotte. Will participation be compulsory?"

"I wish it could be. But I don't think there's any way to enforce that. People of all denominations are welcome in our beautiful state. If they don't like it, they should move. Westcarolina will be the nation's first experience with a godly state. People can vote me out in two years if they choose."

"We've heard something about you hosting 'wild parties' with a large component of sex and drugs. Is there any truth to that?"

"Absolutely not," King said with an indignant expression. "I'm sure that came from my enemies. Our parties are beautiful, large events. We can't monitor everyone's behavior."

"Will you invite me to one?" Annie asked with a mischievous smile.

"I'll have to think about that."

"What about the bombing of the Lenogue clinic?" Annie said, launching into another controversial line of questioning. "There are lots of rumors. Did you or your church have anything to do with that?"

"We try to follow all laws. I can't take responsibility for something that renegade members of God's Gift or other pro-life activists might or might not have done," King said. "I know about it mostly from reading the newspaper."

Annie thought that was a weak answer, so she tried to press him further, but he was adamant about not taking any blame.

"What does the God's Gift ministry do to raise money?"

"We have lots of ventures," he answered with pride. "We've bought some high-rise apartment buildings, a strip shopping center, and property for our residential subdivisions. Our members tithe and we have quite a few wealthy donors. If they do it right, churches can develop property without endangering their tax-exempt status."

After answering a few more questions, King looked at his Rolex watch and said he'd have to stop for another appointment. He urged her to return when he had more time.

"Come to me if you have other questions. I will make sure you have total access. There's no newspaper near Westcarolina that's as large or has the influence of the *Press*. When we do something new, we want you to know about it."

"Thank you," Annie said. "We will treat you and your church fairly, though you may not like all of our coverage."

"I doubt I will. But if it's fair, I'll try not to complain. I know you have a hard job. I've already found that the appetite for news coming out of Westcarolina is insatiable. We get reporters calling from around the world, but there's nothing like the hometown paper."

"Well, I'm sure that you'll see Jim or me a lot," she said.

"Don't be a stranger, Annie," he said, smiling. "And take care of that baby of yours."

CHAPTER 12

After Annie had gone, two men eagerly joined King in his office. One was lieutenant governor Henry Fullspear and the other, more surprising, one was Rob Ryland.

King was eager to hear the opinions of his top two officials. He especially wanted to hear what Rob had to say. He'd hired the Texan a few months previously as his top aide, and knew that Rob had once worked with Annie.

Rob, a fresh-faced man in his thirties, resembled a young choirboy, King thought. As a co-leader of the Nation of Texas, Rob had worked to take over state government and make Texas an independent nation.

King had met Rob at a Nation of Texas fundraiser in Charlotte. King had talked to him at length and found out that Rob's power in the organization had diminished with changes in the top ranks. King promptly offered Rob a job as his chief of staff. The West Texan, recognizing that Westcarolina leadership was a once-in-a-lifetime opportunity, accepted.

King didn't know all of Rob's secrets, however. For instance, Rob hadn't told King that before he rose to leadership in the violent secessionist group, Annie Price had mentored him at the *Houston Times*. Rob had always reflected fondly on that year. As a top investigative reporter, Annie had taught him a lot. She had covered the secessionist movement with Rob's help until she found out he had joined the secessionists and was their spy.

Rob had a darker history with Annie that he'd never tell King.

When Rob and the secessionists secretly arranged an "accident" that had killed Annie's best friend, newspaper staffers assembled at a local bar for a wake. A few hours later, Rob could see that Annie was drunk and offered to take her home. She agreed and when they got to her house, he capitalized on her vulnerable state by forcing her to the bedroom. Although he'd called what happened next consensual sex, Annie had likened it to rape.

She stopped speaking to him at the office until her editor paired them to cover the secessionists. She didn't protest because, Rob suspected, her drunken state at the bar that night had embarrassed her.

King had allowed him to listen in on the interview because Rob was his right-hand man who also knew Annie. Both King (and secretly Rob and Henry) watched Annie leave King's office. With her lustrous dark hair, wide green eyes, and gorgeous long legs, both King and Rob found her incredibly beautiful. Rob didn't admit it to himself, but he didn't date much anymore because he constantly compared other women to her, finding them wanting. When he found out she'd started work as an investigative reporter for the *Press*, it both thrilled and dismayed him.

King looked forward to spending time with Rob, who shared many of his views. He thought he'd enjoy having someone around who was closer to his age. King's relationship with Henry Fullspear was purely professional, and neither trusted the other. King resented Fullspear's condescending tone and grating opinions and he realized that the lieutenant governor was envious of his charm.

Bugging his office was a convenience that allowed King to blackmail people, if such a drastic move was necessary. It didn't happen often but had proved useful. Rob and Fullspear had listened in on Annie's interview with King from a small, wired room next door.

"I still can't believe that Annie Price is working for the *Charlotte Press*," Rob said. "What a stroke of bad luck for you."

"Why is that?" King said. "She seemed very nice and didn't really press any hardball questions, except to ask about my parties."

"That's because it was a first meeting and she was just assessing you," Rob said. "Believe me, it will get worse."

"I didn't like her at all," Fullspear said quickly. As usual, King thought, he was trying to monopolize a subject he knew nothing about.

"I could help you arrange an accident," Rob said after some thought. "That's what we did with her best friend in Houston who'd gotten a little too nosy. We could do something that wouldn't kill Annie, just scare her."

"Oh, that would be a great way to start out," King said with sarcasm. "Scare the preeminent reporter at the *Charlotte Press*? You think the legislature wouldn't suspect us?"

"I tell you, she's poison. Everything she touches becomes a disaster."

"We're already in potentially terrible trouble with the bombing of the Lenogue factory," King said. "I've denied it several times, but I don't think anyone really believes me."

"Well, your people did it, right?" Rob said. "Maybe it would be a show of strength just to admit it."

King said that wasn't possible when he and Henry had just two years to prove themselves before they'd run for election. Besides, the bombing was a felony, especially since it involved the deaths of two guards. Better to stay far away from it. Rob played down the consequences, but King thought it reflected the difference in their interest groups. The Nation of Texas would have immediately claimed credit for such a drastic action and their control of West Texas would have provided them with protection.

"We are in a delicate situation with the legislature," Fullspear added. "They want the political advantages of two new conservative U.S. senators, but some of the more liberal legislators are very unhappy about the creation of Westcarolina."

For once, King thought, Fullspear had said something meaningful without blathering on.

"We try not to kill anyone," King said. "The factory guards' deaths were an anomaly. God's Gift finds many other ways to achieve its objectives. Besides, Annie is pregnant, and I will not kill an innocent fetus. Who's the father, anyway?"

"She's been dating two Texans for a while," Rob said. "One's a former secessionist and a big cattle rancher in West Texas, the other a rich lawyer in Austin."

"Sounds like you have more than a passing interest in her," King said. "Wouldn't you rather kiss her than kill her?"

Rob laughed. "How'd you know she's pregnant?"

"Sometimes I just know these things," King said. "I don't know how, but I'm usually right."

"Well, keep a close eye on her," Rob said. "She's probably the most dangerous woman in the Carolinas."

CHAPTER 13

King Avery's announcement that she was pregnant had shocked Annie, but she knew it was a possibility. She bought a pregnancy test, and it turned up positive. Just to be sure, she followed it up with a quick doctor's appointment. Now, what should she do?

Part of her was irritated that she had been lax about contraception on the romantic night she and Jake Satterfield had spent together in Houston. But another part of her felt jubilant because she'd thought she'd never have a child. She'd dated a lot of men during the last 20 years, but none had seemed right to marry, much less be a father to any children she might have. For a while in her late thirties, she'd thought about adopting a child on her own, but had thrown herself into her work instead.

Before Jake, that is. The more she thought about it, the more she warmed to the idea of having a child with him. Jake was an experienced father of two girls and a boy, and she knew he loved his children beyond measure. That was also potentially a detriment. Could he love another child with three to parent already? In her heart, she thought he could make room for their baby. He was a good person, especially where it concerned children.

But there was also the considerable obstacle of his pending divorce. Annie knew it was imminent, but would he be ready to marry again so soon? Did she really want to marry him—or anyone else right now? Should she consider raising the child on her own? She knew that she'd rather have a two-parent family for the baby. Being a single parent was hard. Women who'd had that responsibility always seemed tired and stressed out. Since she was working at a new job, it would be doubly difficult.

Annie realized that as much as she'd flirted with the idea of marrying Tom Marr, she'd never stopped loving Jake since she'd met him seven years previously. She'd always assumed that a future with Jake wouldn't happen because he and she were never available at the same time. Just when they were getting to know each other, he got his estranged wife pregnant and stayed with her until the little boy was four. By that time, she was dating Tom Marr.

Jake made her laugh and often challenged her view of the world. He was bright, ambitious, and a wonderful lover. He'd be a superb partner in life if things worked out.

It all made her head whirl, and she decided she'd wait a day or two to tell him. She needed to explore her feelings more thoroughly.

Already, her body felt slightly different. Her breasts were sore, and she was more tired than usual. She was moody and out of sorts, and she attributed those feelings to early pregnancy.

She played with her cats for a while, trying to decide what to fix for supper. What she really wanted was a glass of Chardonnay, but she was going to be healthy during her pregnancy. She finally settled on a peanut butter and banana sandwich, reasoning that it had a decent amount of protein.

She'd almost finished her spartan meal when her cell phone rang. She picked it up and realized it was Tom Marr, calling from his ranch.

"Hey, darlin'," he said in the Texas drawl she loved so well. "How's the job? Have you put anybody in prison yet?"

"No, but it's early days," Annie said, responding to his playful mood.

"What's new with you, Tom?"

"I just bought a few more acres to the south of the ranch so we can graze more cattle. Beef prices are at an all-time high, as you may have heard."

"How's Betsy?" She was always interested in Tom's daughter.

"She's thriving at UT, made lots of friends and loves her classes," he said. "She's even thinking about becoming a journalist."

"Lord help her. She's got the chops."

"She made the honor roll for the first semester and she's thinking about pledging a sorority."

Annie was glad to hear a positive report on the girl she'd become close to as she rescued her from trouble in Houston. She knew she'd forever have Tom's gratitude for her actions.

"But I didn't call to discuss Betsy," he said. "I miss you. I thought I'd fly up this weekend if you're not doing anything."

"I've missed you, too. But there's something serious I've got to discuss."

"I'm all ears," he said.

"I hate to tell you over the phone, but I'm pregnant." She held her breath, waiting for Tom to explode or hang up on her. He was a great guy but had an unpredictable temper.

The silence stretched for a minute or two before he said in a strangled voice, "Who's the father?"

"Jake Satterfield," she said. "I know you've had your issues with him, but please cut me some slack."

"You're breakin' my heart," he said in a shaky voice. "I thought you loved me."

"I love you, Tom," she said. "I didn't plan this."

"Have you told that bastard yet?" He was sounding angry. "You know he's a playboy and a jerk. I doubt that he'll do right by you."

"I haven't talked to him yet, but I will shortly."

"Will you marry him?" Tom sounded scornful.

"I don't know. I'm not sure what I want. We'll have to discuss it. As you know, long-distance relationships are hard."

"Hell, if he doesn't want to get married, I'll marry you. Can I keep in touch with you?"

"Of course. Only if you promise you'll date and actively look for someone to love."

"I found her, but it won't be the fairy-tale ending I'd hoped for," he said.

Annie dissolved into tears. It was hard for her to speak. He was such a good man. Why couldn't she love him the way she loved Jake? In some ways, it would make life so much simpler.

"Bye, Tom," she got out before crying and hanging up the phone.

CHAPTER 14

A day later, Annie decided she'd waited long enough to tell Jake about the pregnancy. Tom's words had haunted her. Maybe he would want nothing to do with her or the child. She shivered in her black blazer–better to know anything upsetting now so she could make plans. In her heart, she doubted whether Jake would say anything negative, even though the news would surprise him. He was one of the kindest persons she knew.

She waited until she was home for the day and had a small glass of chardonnay first. Despite her resolve not to drink, she reasoned she needed a little extra courage for this call. She settled herself at her tiny bar in the kitchen.

He answered promptly on the second ring and said he was relieved to hear from her. He tended to call twice a week, but said he'd had trouble getting her.

"I was about to send out the Texas Rangers to look for you," he joked.

"Sorry, I've been busy with work and a few other unanticipated things."

"Tell me about it. I hope nothing it's nothing bad."

"I'm pregnant, Jake. And it's your baby."

He was quiet for a moment, apparently absorbing the news. Her heart thrummed as she waited for him to say something.

"What do you want to do?"

"I want to have the baby. At 42, this is probably the only chance I'll have."

"Well, in that case, 'Will you marry me, Annie Price?'"

"Are you asking me because you think you should, or because you really want to get married?"

"It's not that I'm eager to get married again right away. But I want to marry you and I want our baby."

"In that case, yes. I'm happy to marry you. I love you. You're not sorry about all this, are you?"

"No, sweetie," he said. "We'll have to wait a few weeks; my divorce is almost final. You know this won't be simple, don't you?"

"How can we make it work? I know that you have a job and personal responsibilities in Austin, and I just started an excellent job here. I don't want to leave."

"Well, as a partner in my firm, I can do most of my work remotely. I can't say anything yet, but I have major business coming up in Charlotte. I get my kids every other weekend, so I'll fly down and take full advantage of that. Spending time with them is non-negotiable."

"I agree. Since you still own that Austin condo, you have a ready-made place to stay with them," she said.

"One other thing that concerns me. Women love you and vice versa. Are you ready to give up dating for me?"

"Yes. You don't know how ready I am. I've had designs on you for years, baby. Are you sure you can leave Mr. West Texas high and dry?"

"Of course. Tom knows I'm pregnant and took it very well. You underrate him. He's a good man."

"Well, start planning a tiny wedding."

"Where should we get married?"

"Shouldn't it be in Houston?" he said. "I know your longtime friends from the paper would love to be there."

"Should we send out invitations?"

"Whoa, girl. Got to make sure my divorce is final first."

"Sure. Maybe I'll send out something very simple to about fifty people."

"Fifty?" Jake sounded shocked.

"Okay, I'll think about that more," she said.

"Well, more importantly, how do you feel?

"So far, I'm okay. But I'm just over a month pregnant. I'm tired and have a little morning sickness."

"It sounds like the baby will be born in October," Jake said.

"Yeah. Are four kids too much for you?"

"Baby, you know I'm crazy about kids," he said. "Especially, I'll be so happy having one with you. I love you, Annie Price."

"I love you too, Jake."

CHAPTER 15

She bought a simple, long white dress with an empire design that flattered her pregnancy-swollen breasts. Jake wore a dark blue designer suit and a red tie when they recited their vows six weeks after he first proposed. The words, written together, expressed their resolve for a relationship based on love, respect and equality.

The wedding took place in Houston in the small chapel of an Episcopal church. Besides longtime friends in Houston, relatives and friends from other parts of Texas and Virginia were there. Jake's children—ten-year-old Ashley, eight-year-old Hayley and five-year-old Jason—also attended. Annie paid special attention to her new stepchildren and her parents, who'd traveled from southwest Virginia. All five seemed dubious about the union.

She, on the other hand, was happier than she had a right to be. Jake and his baby to come—how could she get any luckier? A smile wreathed her face during the short ceremony, and she felt suffused by wellbeing.

The reception was festive, with lots of loving speeches, and an almond cake festooned with flowers. Annie made the rounds among the guests. Most said they really missed her and were especially gracious about the pregnancy. Her best friends knew that she'd longed for a baby for years.

Annie and Jake slipped away after a while, with promises to come back often for visits. Her guests asked a lot of questions about her reporting in Westcarolina, and Annie obliged eagerly. Houston was unusually quiet at the moment, and some of her reporting friends were hungry for good stories.

They had no time for a honeymoon after their small wedding. They could spend only one night together before she had to fly back to Charlotte. Jake had chosen one of Annie's favorite boutique hotels, the Magnolia Houston. On Texas Avenue downtown, it featured a modern, eclectic style, yet felt romantic.

Before a developer purchased the paper's headquarters in a multi-million-dollar sale and imploded it, the *Houston Times* used to be near it. Annie missed the imposing white building, but she still loved that part of downtown. It was a treat to stay at the Magnolia.

Annie thought with nostalgia about what had brought her and Jake to this place. She'd met him at a legislative committee session. Maddie, her newspaper friend, who usually covered the meeting and its members, had asked her to do it while Maddie was on vacation. After Annie had filed her story, she'd joined all the journalism and political people who'd gathered at the hotel bar. She'd caught the eye of Jake, who talked to her for several hours. There was a chemistry between them she'd never felt with anyone else.

Since he was Maddie's source and not hers, she felt she could date him, violating no journalism ethics. She quietly checked it out with her editor, and he agreed with some caveats. He knew that reporters sometimes dated a newspaper's sources but insisted that another person on their team actively cover him.

Now Jake was married to Annie. She could hardly believe it, given what they'd both been through. After she got shot on the job, he'd showered her with attention. But he knew by that time, she was also dating Tom Marr. Since she'd told the West Texan she was pregnant by Jake, Annie hadn't heard from Marr again. Which is as it should be, but she still felt sad about him.

She and Jake were making the most of their one-day honeymoon. After settling in the large beige-and-white suite, Jake popped the cork of a bottle of the best champagne, a pricey wedding-night treat. He filled a large glass for himself and offered Annie a small portion.

"Should I drink that?" Annie asked.

"I don't think a small glass will hurt you or the baby," he said. "That's what the obstetrician told us, anyway."

"I guess your ex-wife knows I'm pregnant. Is she upset that you're remarrying?"

"Well, since she's marrying my former law partner after seeing him behind my back for a long time, she has no right to be upset. She's more concerned about the kids, but I intend to keep on being a good father to them."

"I know you will be. That's one reason I'm looking forward to having a baby with you."

She smiled as she held up a short, lacy black negligee for his inspection.

"Look what I bought for our wedding night," she said.

"Hey, Beautiful. That's a lovely gown, but you won't need it tonight."

It turned out she didn't.

The next day, Jake took her to Houston Hobby Airport to catch the short flight to Charlotte. He held her for a long time, and she surprised herself by shaking with sobs. She didn't know how she could function without him, now that they'd been so close during the wedding and honeymoon.

"Sweetie, don't cry. You know I'll be flying to Charlotte in a few weeks, after spending time with the kids and wrapping up some business."

"Yeah. I guess the pregnancy hormones have made me weepy."

"I know they have."

He smoothed her dark French braid and touched her face. "It's okay. I'm looking forward to a wonderful life with you and the baby wherever we are. Don't you forget it."

She smiled and waved goodbye.

CHAPTER 16

Annie was getting a cup of coffee in the newsroom break room when she got a call from a Catholic priest.

"I'm Father James Mikulsky," he said. "Do you have time to meet with me about a Westcarolina church tax proposal?"

"Yes, definitely," Annie said. "Are you in town?"

"Yes, not far from your building. Can you meet at St. Peter Catholic Church on Tryon Street near you? My church is in Kings Mountain, close to Gastonia, but I'm in the big city today on business."

"I can be there in fifteen minutes."

Annie had heard a rumor that Westcarolina was going to tax other denominations and independent churches to benefit God's Gift Church and the new state. King hadn't announced that change, hoping, she thought, to fly under the radar. She wondered if he'd continue to employ such sneaky tactics. She'd better stay on her toes.

When she got to St. Peter, she spent a few minutes enjoying its ambience. According to a plaque, Catholics had built the brick church in 1893. The sanctuary wasn't large, but it had beautiful stained-glass windows and a distinctive altar painting depicting Christ's loaves and fishes' miracle. She'd heard that the first altar decoration had been a well-loved fresco that had collapsed. She knew the church took the remnants, framed them, and placed them in the lower level of the church in a meeting room.

Annie lit a candle in an alcove in back of the sanctuary. She dropped a few coins in the box, praying that her baby would arrive safely when the time came. She sprinkled a little holy water on her forehead for double protection. Annie hadn't entirely lost her

Catholic school upbringing, but didn't go to Mass. She had a hard time believing all the tenets of her school days, but it was better to be safe than sorry.

She felt soothed after the last few months of almost unbearable tension propelled by acclimating to a new job, deciphering a complex story, finding herself pregnant and starting married life. All these changes were good, but sometimes she woke feeling the weight of her world on her shoulders and in her back. The quiet church reminded her of the richness of her life. She felt determined she would take time each day to express her gratitude in prayer.

Father James appeared and directed her to an office behind the sanctuary. She guessed he was about seventy-five, a little stooped but wearing a welcoming smile and a clerical collar under a worn navy sweater. After a few pleasantries in the office, they began talking about the latest proposal by King Avery.

"Given what he's said in public, the churches weren't really surprised that a tax would be imposed," Father James said. We just didn't expect it to be so much or so soon."

He said he'd heard that the proposal called for smaller churches to be assessed $10,000 a year and larger ones at $20,000 a year.

"Even $10,000 a church would be ruinous for us," Father James said. "We have at least 50 churches in Westcarolina, most with small congregations. The diocese would help us, but it's not wealthy, either."

Larger churches, such as some Methodist and Baptist churches, would also be hurt financially by such rules, he noted.

Many of the churches were quietly protesting but hadn't been able to get King Avery on the phone. Instead, they had talked to Henry Fullspear, the lieutenant governor, or to one of his office staff. Father James said he'd met briefly with Rob Ryland, Avery's new chief of staff, at the God's Gift Charlotte office. Ryland had brushed off his concerns.

"He said most churches would be happy to pay such a tax to operate in such a unique and beautiful new state."

"Rob Ryland works for Westcarolina?" Annie asked. She was incredulous and dismayed. Her hands began shaking so much that she couldn't take decent notes. Surely it wasn't the same man who'd raped her after an alcohol-filled night seven years ago.

"What does he look like?" She asked Father James in a trembling voice.

"He's a nice-looking young man of about thirty-five, with dark hair and a Texas accent. You're from Texas, right? Do you know him?"

"He sounds like someone I knew in Texas, but I don't know why he'd be in North Carolina." Annie knew she had to calm down to finish the interview.

"Actually, he asked whether I'd talked to you," the priest said. "I told him I hadn't talked to anyone in the press. But he gave me the idea of contacting you. Can you do anything for us?"

"I definitely will write about it. When's King Avery supposed to announce it?"

"I heard he was waiting until he'd talked to some bigwigs in the larger churches. I don't think he's prepared the church community for this bombshell. I've never heard of this being done anywhere," Father James said. "I thought in our country there was a firm dividing line between church and state."

"A church or a state shouldn't have–and doesn't have–the power to collect taxes from churches while one gets favorable treatment. Did Rob Ryland say anything else?"

"He said the churches should just consider it the cost of doing business, like any other expense, like buying hymnals or altar cloths," Father James said.

Annie laughed.

"Now that's a good one. I doubt that those minor expenses or any more like it would come close to being the same as what sounds like very burdensome taxes.

"I will talk to you again in a few days, Father James. I need time to talk to other churches as well."

Back at the office, Annie told Jim and Phil what she'd found out from Father James. She also mentioned that King's new chief of staff was Rob Ryland, someone she knew from the Texas secessionist movement.

"He's a terrible person and likely to appeal to King's worse instincts. He bears close watching."

Phil and Jim were aghast at the speed King was moving to institute such a controversial tax. Phil quickly divided up the churches that Annie and Jim needed to call. They wanted to move quickly before the tax was officially announced.

CHAPTER 17

Just before Annie was to call other church officials about the tax proposal, two men stopped by the office to meet her. She told the front desk to send them up.

Jim gave them a warm welcome and Annie could tell that her fellow investigative reporter knew them well.

"Annie, here are two good guys," Jim said. "They fought hard against the establishment of Westcarolina and they're probably the new state's most vocal critics."

Sam Waller, who was of medium height with short brown hair and a pudgy figure, introduced himself as a longtime member of the N.C. Senate. His companion was taller and balding with a quick smile. His name was Ike Hinton, and he told Annie he had been in the N.C. House for 22 years and was the minority leader. It was obvious that they respected Jim and the *Charlotte Press*.

"We opposed Westcarolina, because we knew radical rules that would benefit only God's Gift Church would follow," Ike said. "But King Avery overwhelmingly swayed the legislature with his promise he could deliver two new conservative U.S. senators.

"King is very charming and smart enough to listen to reason," Ike said. "In normal times, we could work with him to make the new state at least palatable.

"The biggest problem is who he surrounds himself with—nasty people like Henry Fullspear and his ilk. Rob Ryland, this new guy from Texas who became King's top aide recently, is really bad news. He is handling the current push to tax churches exorbitant amounts."

Annie, who was standing, felt dismayed all over again, just hearing the name. Was the odious Rob going to follow her around for the rest of her life? She closed her eyes for a moment and shifted her balance. The legislators looked concerned.

"I'm sorry, Annie," Ike said quickly. "Are you going to faint?"

He helped her into a chair, where she quickly regained some color and composure. She still couldn't believe Rob was working for King Avery. King was likely corrupt and stretching his new powers, but she didn't think he was violent and immoral like Rob.

"Sorry, I guess I'm having some pregnancy issues," Annie said.

She added, "I knew Rob back in Texas and he's an awful person. I can't believe he's risen to become King Avery's top aide."

"Perhaps you can fill us in more completely over lunch soon," Sam said. "In the meantime, I know that you've got deadline work looming, so we'll leave you alone. But perhaps next week, we can sit down with you and Jim."

"Definitely," Annie said.

"You can put us on the record as being opposed to the change," Sam said. "It's discriminatory, unconstitutional, and dumb."

Annie wrapped up her conversations with the two state legislators, satisfied with the information she gathered for the explosive story.

The two men left the newsroom and Annie and Jim got busy. They divided up the largest churches in Gastonia and nearby cities, reasoning that God's Gift would have started close to home. They decided it would be quicker and make sense to call more churches, rather than trying to visit them.

The next person Annie talked to was Bernie Barber, minister of a 400-member Baptist church in Gastonia. She explained to Barber why she was calling.

"Oh, yes. We got a visit yesterday from a young man who said our church would be taxed $20,000 a year for the privilege of operating in Westcarolina," Bernie said. "We couldn't believe he was for real. As far as I know, the U.S. Constitution still prohibits establishing a state religion.

"He was very frank with us that the funds would help maintain the activities of God's Gift Church and set up functions of the new government."

"We protested that $20,000 a year was a considerable sum of money for us," Bernie added. "We're not a wealthy church and that money was pledged to fix a leaky roof. The young man essentially said he didn't care about our problems and if we didn't like it, we could always move out of Westcarolina."

Annie called a prominent Methodist church in Blowing Rock and got much the same story.

The minister, James Winters, said he'd gotten a phone call two days earlier that essentially threatened his church with vandalism if it didn't pay the $20,000 owed by June.

"I told the man that we'd never been charged before for normal church activities, and he said Westcarolina was going to be different. The preeminent church was God's Gift and people would be encouraged to join it, rather than stay with the old denominations."

"Did the man who called introduce himself?" Annie asked.

"He told me his name, but I don't remember it. I got the impression that members of God's Gift Church congregations had been pressed into service."

Annie and Jim looked at each other after the call to the Methodist church ended.

"If we finish up fairly quickly, we can write a story tomorrow for Sunday's paper," Annie said.

CHAPTER 18

Annie and Jim decided that since she'd gotten an early start, Annie would be the lead reporter on the church tax story.

She worked quickly, weaving in the comments from the church officials she'd talked to. Jim stayed on the phone getting a few more.

One church he called was the AME Crossroads Church near Morganton. With a predominantly Black congregation, it had little use for the evangelical, mostly white empire of King Avery's God's Gift Church.

Reggie Brown, pastor of AME Crossroads, was so upset that Annie could hear every word he spoke to Jim as he vowed that the church wouldn't pay the $20,000 Henry Fullspear had said it owed.

"My church is made up of hard-working people who can barely make it from week to week. Who does he think he is, God? I knew the state legislature was making a big mistake by creating Westcarolina. King Avery uses the church as a cover for his attention-seeking behavior and greedy actions."

Jim incorporated the comments he had received, including those and others, into their main story. Annie was impressed by how well they worked together. Sometimes, two reporters just didn't mesh the way she and Jim did.

Early on, Annie had called the office of King Avery to get reaction on the widespread opposition to the tax. His secretary, a nice older woman named Marge Carroll, asked if Annie could come by their Charlotte office. Since it was just a few blocks from the newspaper headquarters, she thought that was a good idea. It was usually better to talk to primary sources in person than over the phone because you could observe their body language.

She arrived at the 10th floor office just prior to 4 p.m., two hours before her first deadline. She wished she'd insisted on meeting King earlier. Her hands felt icy, and she dreaded the thought of the heated confrontation that was bound to happen.

No sooner had she gotten off the elevator than Rob Ryland greeted her.

"Annie, I was hoping I'd see you again," he said with faux joy. She shrank back a couple of steps, consumed with distaste. He held out his arms to hug her and she sidestepped the embrace.

"I don't understand why you're here. Isn't ruining one state enough? Why did you leave the Nation of Texas? I thought you were the co-leader," Annie said.

"Things change. A big bitch of a woman who thought she knew everything took some of the main functions from me. It was either kill her or leave."

Annie guessed he probably wasn't joking but didn't want to pursue it further.

"Pregnancy becomes you," he said, checking her out up and down.

Annie had worn a stretchy beige dress with some nice turquoise jewelry she'd bought on a visit to Santa Fe. She found it was hard to dress well in the early stages of pregnancy because maternity clothes were still too big and regular clothes were mostly too small.

"Who's the father, anyway?" Rob asked with a smile that never reached his eyes. "Hope you're not birthing a bastard. I'd be disappointed in you."

"I'm married to Jake Satterfield," she said pointedly. "You wouldn't dare say such things if he were here."

"Ah, the Austin millionaire lawyer," he said with an ironic laugh. "You've done all right for yourself, Annie. Better watch it, though. I hear he loves the women, especially a certain TV anchor."

Annie tried unsuccessfully to get out of Rob's way. She shuddered when he took her arm to lead her. She pulled it away. Annie couldn't stand to be near him.

"I'm supposed to escort you to King's inner sanctum," he said. "We can spend more time reacquainting ourselves later. I hear that pregnant women are especially good in bed. Want to continue where we left off a few years ago?"

"You're disgusting," she said, her voice trembling with anger. "You forced me, and I should have reported it."

"Ah, but then your drinking habits would come out."

"Do you want me to brief King Avery about your vile comments? I suspect that as a man of the cloth, he'd think twice about having you as his chief of staff," Annie said, fending off a feeling she'd vomit at any moment. It would serve him right if she threw up all over his designer shoes.

"Okay, okay. Can't you take a little teasing?"

She didn't deign to answer.

By this time, they'd reached King's office, and the pastor stood up to greet her.

"Annie, you look marvelous. I heard you expect the little boy in about seven months," King said.

"Are you sure it's a boy?" Annie asked. She thought that King's charm was undeniable.

"That's what my instinct says, but I'm not infallible. He grinned and offered her a chair. Rob quickly disappeared from the room.

"You know I've come to talk to you about the tax on churches. I've talked to a lot of churches and some state officials, and they all say it's akin to setting up a government religion, which is unconstitutional."

"I know they're angry about it, so I've decided to abandon the idea," King said.

His words shocked her into silence for a beat or two. She felt nauseated again, thinking of all the work they'd put into their reporting.

"I don't understand. You've contacted dozens of churches and presented it as a done deal," she said.

"Well, it was more like a trial balloon. We wanted to assess the opinions out there. Since churches and North Carolina officials feel so strongly against it, we've dropped it. There are other ways to raise money to support God's Gift and the new state."

"Like what?"

"All in good time. Whatever we do, I'm sure you'll find out and write about it."

"Yeah, that's what reporters do," she said.

"Well, this initiative could have brought in tens of thousands of dollars," he said. "But I'm not blaming you."

His tone of voice and steely look belied his words. But Annie was used to having subjects of stories complain about them. Her reporter's armor, honed after many years, came in handy in situations like this.

"It was your mistake, not mine." She forced a smile to take some of the sting out of her words. It was too early to make him the kind of enemy who wouldn't talk to her.

Outside his office, she quickly called Jim and gave him the news.

"This is going to be a lot of work, totally redoing the story," she said. "Can you ask for a later deadline?"

CHAPTER 19

Since Annie and Jake's wedding was small and took place in faraway Houston, she didn't invite anyone from the Charlotte newspaper. She'd started strongly with her beat and hadn't had time to make friends. The exception was Sarah Simonds. Sarah was originally from Dallas, understood Texas politics and those of North Carolina, and kept Annie up to date on newsroom happenings. Annie liked her a lot and made time to stop by her desk and chat at least a few times a week. Sarah was petite with streaked brown hair, not exactly beautiful, but with a lovely smile.

Annie's friend wasn't married. Sarah was one of the few staffers Annie had told when she found out she was pregnant and obsessing about it. The reporter said she was envious because she wanted to become a mother before it was too late. Like Annie, Sarah had thought about becoming a single mother, but so far, had taken no steps. Though she longed for marriage and a child, she couldn't have been any nicer about Annie's situation.

She stopped by Annie's desk one day to chat and made an unexpected suggestion.

"I want to give you and Jake a post-wedding party. You've never been properly introduced to the staff and become part of our party set. I'm sure Jake must be climbing the walls with his job here."

"That's a lovely idea. I'll talk about it to Jake tonight."

Annie found it surprising how smoothly Jake had transitioned to Charlotte and started working remotely. He was working on some projects he said he'd tell Annie about soon. A lot of his work dealt with businesses in trouble, and she knew he had to keep it confidential.

There were a few downsides. Annie's little house was so compact that she didn't see how they would manage once the baby came. Jake was using the second bedroom as his office, and it was the smaller of the two.

"We'll definitely have to buy a new house," he said. "But we'll stay near uptown, so you won't have a long commute."

Jake began studying the real estate offerings and became drawn to large two-story dwellings in prestigious areas such as Eastover and Myers Park, with pools and luxurious outdoor patio kitchens. Annie thought some were a little ostentatious, but she didn't say that. If that's what he wanted, she'd approach it with an open mind.

"Just as long as it's not a 12-bedroom mountain house like King Avery's," she said.

"I doubt that there are many of those in Charlotte. Maybe a few at Lake Norman or Lake Wylie."

"The lakes are nice, but a long commute for your aging wife."

"Honey, you're in your prime and don't you forget it." He grinned and kissed her.

They'd tried to explore more of Charlotte and Westcarolina, but such excursions had proved more of a goal than action. Trips were difficult with Annie's punishing work schedule and Jake's trips to Austin every other weekend to spend with his kids. She missed him when he left, but sometimes she enjoyed the solitude of a quiet weekend. She'd read and do chores like wash clothes. Jake was splendid company, but his powerful personality could wear her out if she'd had a hard day. Her pregnancy was taking a lot out of her.

She told Jake about Sarah's plan to host a party for them and he predictably was pleased.

"You're just a party boy at heart," she said, teasing him.

"Nothing wrong with that."

The night of the party, Annie had a hard time deciding what to wear. She settled on black pants with a loose-fitting maroon top and some gold jewelry.

She thought Jake looked great in black jeans and his leather bomber jacket. He'd let his hair grow a little, and it made him look younger than his forty-five years. Annie was proud to be seen with him.

That pride lasted about an hour, she thought sourly, as she watched him flirt, first with Sarah, then with practically every other female at the party.

She noted he spent the most time with Laura Stanton, a junior reporter with long blonde hair, blue eyes and a red blouse with eye-popping cleavage. She was a general assignment reporter with blatant attempts to move to the investigative desk.

She wondered what Laura and Jake were talking about for so long. Finally, she went over and made it clear in a subtle way that there were other people he needed to meet. She felt like the bad mom chiding the little boy. It wasn't a good feeling.

"You've been keeping this handsome guy under wraps, Annie," Laura said. "You need to bring him out more often."

Jake looked gratified by the attention.

"Laura was telling me about her terrific stories on traffic problems. She said they've gotten a lot of feedback from the state transportation board."

"That's right," Annie said evenly. "Laura has done some good work."

Laura seemed disappointed when Annie escorted Jake across the living room at Sarah's house to meet some of the other Press staffers.

The rest of the evening continued in the same vein. Annie noticed that while he talked to the men, he kept drifting back to the female reporters, especially the younger, more attractive ones. She could feel herself getting angry, a slow burn that was spoiling the evening for her.

She tried to immerse herself in her conversations with staffers but was glad when most partygoers had left. She'd felt obliged to stay till the end.

She and Jake both gave Sarah hugs and thanked her profusely. Annie had brought her friend wine and flowers.

Annie drove, because it was obvious that Jake had had too much wine to get them home safely. She was silent, trying to figure out how to express her anger calmly.

"What's wrong, baby?" Jake asked as they undressed. "You're awfully quiet."

"I didn't like it when you spent so much time talking to Laura and the other younger, attractive women. I'm a 42-year-old pregnant woman. I can't compete with cute 25-year-olds for your attention."

"Sweetie, you don't have to compete with anyone. I married you because you're beautiful, smart, savvy, and you're carrying our baby."

"That's all well and good, Jake. But when you spend the bulk of your time at a party talking to a young woman whose breasts are spilling out of her tacky low-necked top, it doesn't make me feel good."

"Annie, you know me," Jake said with an air of impatience. "I like talking to pretty women. I also enjoy talking to homely women and unattractive men. I've always been a people person. I can't change that, and I don't want to change. You need to lighten up."

Annie looked in the mirror at her burgeoning figure and felt like crying. A few stray tears rolled down her cheeks before she could stop them.

"Oh, baby. Come here and let me show you how much I appreciate you."

His lovemaking was tender and comforting, but she couldn't let go of the impression that he was trying to pacify her instead of satisfying her grievance.

The next morning, she still felt bruised by his behavior at the party. Despite loving him dearly, she wondered if she could tolerate the attention he directed to attractive women.

CHAPTER 20

King was working in his office at the Blowing Rock mansion when Claire stuck her head in the door.

"Got a minute?" she said, walking in and taking a seat across from him. He inwardly groaned. Claire's minutes often turned into hours and involved subjects he'd rather not think about.

Today wasn't quite as bad.

"We need to start planning our summer party," she said. "The invitations should go out soon."

"Yeah, I know. They discussed timing and decided that the latter part of June would work well.

"Can you take charge of the guest list and catering?" King said. "I'll approve the guest list before the invitations go out."

"Of course. I'll check in with you when I finish."

He noticed dispassionately that her short blonde hair, combed in her usual spiked style and heavily gelled, looked at odds with her conservative outfit, as usual. He wondered if she'd be getting a tattoo next.

He wished he really cared, but sadly, whatever passion their marriage had possessed, was long gone. Claire used their big parties to find her latest lover, starting a relationship that lasted a few months.

Her current lover was a young software mogul from Raleigh who'd contributed millions of dollars to God's Gift Church. Claire was pushing 46, but she looked as good as she did in her thirties. She supported the church with some of her inherited millions, instead of hands-on charitable activities many pastors' wives would lead. That financial support was vital to God's Gift, so he guessed they'd be yoked for life.

They'd been married for 15 years. King originally thought having a baby or two might cement their union, but Claire had made it clear from the beginning that she didn't want children. He'd given up with no fight. He didn't want to be what would amount to a single parent.

He dreaded the parties but recognized that they showcased the church and brought in plenty of money because of contributions that came with them. He found little to care about among the wealthy people, mostly couples, who attended. They came out of curiosity about the big house and sometimes a sexual element subtly fostered by Claire. He knew some of the bedrooms were occasionally used for clandestine purposes.

Because he was handsome and charismatic, there should be no end of possibilities for his non-Claire love life. Currently, however, there was only one woman who attracted him, and he'd probably never act on his interest.

The person he was currently attracted to, surprisingly, was Annie Price, the new reporter for the *Charlotte Press*. Ever since their first meeting, when he'd sensed her pregnancy, he'd felt protective of her. Every time he saw her now, with her swelling abdomen, just added to that feeling. Since King would never have children with Claire, he valued women who were willing, even looked forward, to being mothers. He knew it was ridiculous to care for Annie, because she had the power and the intelligence to destroy him and the church he'd founded. But there was something so pure about her search for the truth.

She was nice-looking, but besides her imposing height, wasn't nearly as striking as Claire. Unlike Claire, she'd probably be faithful to her husband and encourage him to be a better man. King was curious about her new husband and had asked Rob more about him. Rob dismissed him and his success as a Texas lawyer, but he sensed some envy there. There was a strange vibe between Rob and Annie that he didn't quite understand. He knew they'd worked together at Annie's Houston newspaper during a time Rob was secretly becoming active in the secessionist movement. Perhaps that's where the animus started.

King wondered what it would be like to be a reporter. He thought he'd be good at it, because he had a lot of curiosity about things. But he'd never had a chance to escape his destiny as an evangelical minister.

His father had no aptitude for the ministry, nor did his older brother, Keith, who was a San Francisco banker. King thought Keith was gay–he wanted nothing to do with religion. Keith almost never came back to North Carolina. King sensed that his high school years had been very tough. He wasn't particularly handsome, nor did he excel at anything. King suspected his brother was bullied, but he was so busy with his grandfather's ministry that he didn't really know.

King's mother seemed mostly disinterested in her grown sons after raising them. The only thing she seemed to be passionate about was growing orchids. King thought she didn't care one way or another about what he did.

It had been thrilling at first, but now the ministry, while time-consuming, didn't excite him much. He was looking to hire more assistant ministers so he could focus on the new state. The gift of Westcarolina from the former president came just in time to give him a new beginning. But was he capable of doing all the things that needed to be done? He hoped so.

CHAPTER 21

The appearance of Rob interrupted King's thoughts. Since Rob had become King's chief of staff, he'd never bothered to knock unless he knew for sure that King had a visitor. Their business and personal relationship had developed astonishingly fast, to King's gratification. He almost felt like Rob was his alter ego—a risk-taking, take-no-prisoners bad boy.

King felt happier when he was working at his Blowing Rock mansion rather than his less glamorous Charlotte or Gastonia offices. Since they were at the mansion with some free time, he expected Rob to bring up the church tax debacle. It didn't take long. Rob sat in the chair beside King's cluttered desk and leaned forward for emphasis.

"Hey, King. Is this a good time for a post-mortem on the church tax program?"

"The sooner the better," said King, who'd been dreading this moment. "Then we can move on."

"What went wrong, do you think?" Rob said in what King interpreted as a neutral tone.

"I guess I didn't realize just how negative the reactions would be. Annie Price and her partner interviewed a lot of ministers and were about to write an extremely unfavorable story."

"You can't be overly sensitive to Annie and her so-called journalism," Rob said with the belligerent tone he used when talking about his former investigative partner. "She's going to find fault with us always. You'll see. I think you're a marshmallow where Annie is concerned."

"That's unfair. She had the goods on us from every denomination in Westcarolina. Remember, even though the North Carolina

General Assembly and Congress have approved us, we still have to pass muster before the next election."

"We shouldn't worry about them," Rob said. "They're thrilled at the thought of two more conservative senators. The Republicans are in the majority again and they're salivating about Westcarolina. We can do anything.

"Maybe you should have preached about this in the pulpit to give more reasons churches could benefit from it, especially funding joint mission trips to Africa and South America," he added.

"You're probably right. I just didn't think it through." King's glumness about the subject warned Rob off.

"Well, everyone makes mistakes. I should have foreseen the trouble and given better advice."

King hoped Rob would bring up something else. He was getting tired of taking the heat for a decision he still believed was the right one. Rob moved on, hitting another sore spot.

"You know I've been trying to befriend Henry Fullspear, your obnoxious lieutenant governor. He's been critical to your pulling back on the church tax. He says you're an extremely weak leader, and he would have gotten those churches in line."

"He did, did he?" King said with more than a touch of anger in his voice. "I don't understand why he's so negative. Lieutenant Governor is hardly a low-level job. But then, his envy has always been just barely concealed."

"I've taken the path you recommended and have looked for discrepancies in his work," Rob said. "There's ample evidence he's been fiddling with some funds in one or two of the church accounts."

"Prepare a report and I'll confront him with it. He makes a fine salary and shouldn't need to do that."

"I've been trying to pay him more attention so I can keep an eye on his work and whatever else he's doing. I must say that he's not much fun to be around. I'll keep trying, though. I hear that he's quite the outdoorsman, so we've talked about spending a guy's day out, doing something manly," Rob said. "Let's have a beer around 5 p.m. and chat about what's coming next."

"That would be great," King said with enthusiasm. "You know how much I depend on you, Rob. I want you to know I've approved a $100,000 bonus for you because of your recent work."

"I really appreciate your generosity," Rob said. "I'll be in my office if you need me before we get together for a beer."

King kept a calm face, but inside he was pleased that Rob seemed happy and grateful. Sometimes his chief aide was hard to read.

Rob's walked out of King's office calmly, but the thought of more money always made him feel giddy. His boss didn't see him take a victory lap through the living room before quietly returning to his work.

King hoped Rob would take at least a temporary leave from the Nation of Texas. He was aware of Rob's dissatisfaction with the way things were going with the rebel group. Because of the mammoth size of Texas, King doubted that Rob's secessionist organization could make it a country of its own. Probably the best the secessionists could hope for would be to control a small area of West Texas.

King didn't know that Annie Price was still Rob's longtime obsession, and he came close to needing to be around her. He wasn't aware that Rob carried a torch for his former newspaper partner.

He also didn't know that Rob secretly thought about killing Annie.

If he couldn't have Annie, nobody should, especially not King. King had no inkling that Rob fit the psychological profile of a narcissistic person who could easily become a killer. The only thing standing in his top aide's way was that Annie was one of his few weaknesses—he couldn't imagine a world without her.

King was ripe for Rob's efforts to flatter and ingratiate himself to the governor and church leader. Who knew what would happen? Though King wasn't aware of it, Rob was looking forward to a much bigger role governing Westcarolina.

CHAPTER 22

Rob had spent all day with Henry Fullspear in the Gastonia office of Westcarolina, trying to learn how God's Gift many accounts were kept.

"Wow, you've done quite a job, Henry," he said, flattering the older man. "It's time for a break, don't you think? I'll grab a couple of beers from King's refrigerator."

"You won't get any argument from me," Henry said.

Rob had a hard time keeping a pleasant look on his face. Just being around Henry irritated him. The lieutenant governor sometimes seemed like he came from another planet, his sense of humor arcane and his interests much narrower than those of Rob or King.

Never mind. If the secessionist movement had taught Rob anything, it was that you didn't necessarily have to like everyone. The important thing was to learn how to use them.

Both Henry and King somehow did double duty in their jobs, which Rob admired. Henry worked hard as lieutenant governor of Westcarolina and the chief financial officer of God's Gift Church. Of course, the church's interests closely aligned with those of the new state. Though Westcarolina was not exactly a theocracy, it came close.

Sitting in Henry's small office felt stifling; downtown Gastonia just depressed him. Like King, he much preferred to be at the Blowing Rock office.

"What's there to do around here?" he asked Henry. "I'll likely be stuck here over the weekend."

"Do you like to hike?"

When Rob nodded, Henry suggested going to Crowder's Mountain State Park, just a few miles down the road and a frequent draw for hikers and mountain climbers.

"Saturday is more likely to be crowded, so we could meet in the parking lot at 7 a.m., do a quick hike to The Pinnacle – that's what they call the summit -- and be back in the office by 11," Henry said.

"That sounds fantastic. Just what I need to shake off the cobwebs," Rob said.

"Great. Don't forget to wear sturdy shoes."

By the time Rob arrived at 7:15 on Saturday, Henry was pacing.

"Sorry I'm a bit late. Had a hard time getting up this early."

"At God's Gift, we're known for punctuality," Fullspear said with an irritated air. "Oh well, let's go."

Rob was annoyed at Fullspear's lecturing tone. He didn't count fifteen minutes as late. Henry would never make it in the ranks of the Texas secessionists, where you had to be endlessly patient and flexible to get anywhere. There was a huge amount of disorganization within its ranks that had to be tolerated. No wonder that the picky Fullspear didn't seem to have any friends.

They'd planned to hike challenging uphill paths to the Pinnacle, about two miles. They moved silently, with a sense of purpose. Rob, never one to notice the beauty of outdoors, couldn't help but appreciate the spring greenness and occasional wildflower in shades of red, yellow or purple.

However, he realized how out of shape he was. How could a hefty middle-aged man have more energy than he did? Rob wasn't used to steep climbs, despite that, he was fitter and over twenty years younger than Fullspear. He had to remind himself that the older man did a lot of hiking and mountain climbing.

"Why don't you go ahead?" Rob said. "I need to rest, and I'll catch up with you in a few minutes."

After about ten minutes, Rob had regained some energy and resumed the hike. Before long, he spied Henry at the top with binoculars.

"This is gorgeous," Rob said. "What a view. Would you take a picture of me at the summit, using my cellphone? I'll send it to some of my secessionist friends."

"Sure. You stand up there and I'll move a little closer to the edge."

Rob smiled for the camera and inspected the result.

"Hmmm. Not as dramatic as I hoped. Let's try a couple more times, maybe with you standing back a little more."

This time Henry stood even closer to the Pinnacle's edge and snapped with Rob's cellphone.

Suddenly, with a fearful and anguished cry, Henry slipped off the mountain and fell hundreds of feet. His helpless screams echoed through the mountain area and curdled Rob's blood.

Rob looked around quickly. A bearded young hiker ran toward him.

"This is awful," the hiker said. "Do you need to use my cellphone to call 911? I also have the ranger's number. He's a friend of mine and was going to meet me here soon."

Despite his dislike of Henry Fullspear, Rob was shocked and shaken by the fall and wondered if he'd be blamed for causing the older man's certain death. Of course, he'd nudged Henry closer to the edge on purpose, to be truthful, and bore responsibility for the catastrophe.

He called 911 and the ranger station. Below them, within a few minutes, he could hear several emergency vehicles screaming to a stop. In about 15 minutes, he and the generous hiker were joined by Chief Ranger Rick Donovan, who seemed sympathetic. They spent a long time talking.

"It's happening more and more," Donovan said. "People with their cellphones are taking too many chances. The same thing is happening in other parks. Recently, a young mother from Charlotte fell to her death here, while she was attempting to take pictures of her husband and three children at the summit. You shouldn't blame yourself too much."

Rob explained to Donovan that the man who fell off the mountain was Henry Fullspear, the lieutenant governor. Henry loved the park and would often go hiking there.

"Oh, boy," Donovan said. "I should prepare for an onslaught by the media."

"Yeah," Rob said. "My boss, King Avery, should do the same. He sleeps in, so I better try to call him.

"I really appreciate what you said. If you tell the media how often cellphone falls are happening, that will go a long way toward getting journalists to understand it," Rob said.

He was perking up and figuring out how to use the tragedy to his advantage. He asked the hiker if he could use his cellphone one more time. King would know what to do.

CHAPTER 23

King Avery allowed himself to sleep late on Saturdays, reasoning that he got up early every other day. He noticed that the other half of the bed remained untouched. He supposed Claire had spent a wild night with the software mogul. King made it a practice of never asking her whereabouts when she was out for the night. He had no appetite for the fight that would follow. Claire would subtly—or straight out—accuse him of being a terrible lover.

Still, it was a lonely way to live and since Claire didn't want a divorce, he reflected gloomily on his depressing future. He was thinking how much Rob had brightened his life when he heard his cellphone ringing from a number he didn't recognize. It was Rob.

"Hey, buddy," King said. "How did the hike go?"

"Not very well. Henry was taking my photograph at the summit when he fell off the mountain and died."

"That's terrible. I wasn't very fond of Henry, but what a bad way to go. Tell me truthfully. Did you plan this? I know you didn't like Henry. Should I worry that the blame will fall on you, then filter up to me?"

"Honestly, no. It just happened, and it shocked me, just like anyone else. I talked to the ranger in charge, and he said falls that take place during cellphone pictures have become increasingly common," Rob said. "The same thing took a young mother recently while she was shooting pictures of her family."

"Praise the Lord. Not because of the unfortunate young woman, but because neither of us will automatically get the blame. It also removes a sticky problem. As you noted and I saw for myself, Henry was stealing from some of the God's Gift Church accounts. It would have created a huge public relations problem to get rid of him," King said.

"I need to get a shower, get dressed and get going. Lots of calls need to be made. Can you get back here soon?"

"Sure, after I get through all the red tape. The police are on their way to interview me. Since I'm using a borrowed cellphone from the park ranger, I need to get off, anyway."

"Don't say anything I wouldn't say to the police."

"Of course not. I'm not a novice at this kind of thing."

King sprang into action, getting out of bed for a luxurious, longer than usual shower. He hummed as he put together an outfit of khakis and a black collared shirt. His off-hours staples of jeans and T-shirts wouldn't do for an occasion as serious as this one, though he'd spend most of his day on the phone.

He castigated himself for his overwhelming feeling of relief. It wasn't a very Christian way to react—he should mourn a close associate, an executive who kept a lot of his secrets. But Henry had been a constant irritant and a clear thief, stealing from God's Gift Church. And King wouldn't have to put up with his caustic criticism again.

He created a list of calls to be made. Chief among them were North Carolina and Congressional officials who were unofficial sponsors of Westcarolina, to let them know that the new state would continue to flourish without Henry. He also had some other ideas he would float.

When Rob showed up a few hours later, looking worn and serious, King pounced on him.

"How'd you like to be the new lieutenant governor?" King asked with a certain amount of glee.

"You mean it?" Rob said. "Would they accept me as a former secessionist leader of Texas?"

"Yes, and yes. Our supporters at the national and state level were emphatic that they'd accept anyone I wanted. I told them I want you."

King smiled broadly, congratulating himself for having pulled off the political feat. Now he'd have a buddy around to share the responsibilities and the fun.

"Of course, you'll have to run for election in a couple of years, but you can spend time before then making a name for yourself."

Rob pasted a big smile on his face and gave King a quick hug. "I'm overcome. I never thought anything like this would happen to me. Do you mind if I walk around the patio for a bit? I need to take this all in."

"Go ahead. I know you've had quite a day."

King watched Rob make his way to the giant stone patio with its elaborate outdoor kitchen. His aide and prospective lieutenant governor walked around, looking at the stunning view. King's mind was whirling, and he needed to calm down. It had been a disturbing but ultimately triumphant day. He would not waste any more sympathy on Henry.

King had been upfront about his feelings. He'd hinted more than once that if Henry were out of the picture, he'd like nothing better than to elevate Rob to the lieutenant governor's job. Now it was happening and only good would come out of it.

Rob would stand strongly behind him, even take the lead sometimes, for reforms and truly turn Westcarolina into what it should be–a revolutionary place where the whims of an individual would become secondary to the needs of the state. They could clean up the unsavory parts of society that hampered most cities and rural areas and make sure most Westcarolians were loyal to God's Gift Church.

It was all because of Henry falling off a mountain. Not that he hadn't had a little help. King didn't believe Rob about the purported accident. He was almost certain that when Rob had told Henry to move back toward the edge to get a better picture, he'd known what would happen. He was just surprised that his chief of staff wouldn't admit it.

King permitted himself a small smile. A sticky problem was gone.

CHAPTER 24

Annie and Jim were talking quietly about their next story when a news bulletin was issued by one of the local television stations. As in most newsrooms, big-screen TVs were plentiful.

They listened intently as the TV reporter told of Lieutenant Governor Henry Fullspear's fatal accident on Crowders Mountain. The story quoted the chief ranger discussing how accidental cellphone camera deaths were increasing. Then it mentioned Fullspear's climbing companion: Rob Ryland, Gov. Kingston Avery's top staffer. The story made it clear that Rob wasn't to blame.

"Oh, yeah?" Annie said to Jim. She'd told him plenty of stories about Rob. She didn't believe he was innocent in Fullspear's death. She felt chagrined that he was still in Westcarolina—he was invading her space, just as he did in Texas.

They quickly called up the more current and detailed Associated Press story on the incident to learn more than the TV bulletin had included.

"Listen to this, Annie," Jim said. The story also highlighted how King Avery had nominated Rob to succeed Fullspear as lieutenant governor and it received approval until the next election cycle.

Annie felt flabbergasted. On the TV station, Rob was promising to build on Fullspear's legacy by making Westcarolina the envy of all states. The story mentioned Rob's former leadership of the Texas secession movement. Rob said the fight was "in excellent hands" and he was "ready for a new challenge."

Rob had lived for the secession struggle, Annie thought. What was he up to? His lack of credentials for a high-level state job stunned her. What did he plan to do? She knew it would benefit Rob and probably hurt a lot of Westcarolina residents. Annie was worried and wondered what it meant for her reporting future. She hoped Jim would keep covering the lieutenant governor's office.

She and Jim went into reporting mode to get a meaty story ready for the website and the following day's paper.

"I'm going to call the two couples I met a while back for their reactions," Annie told Jim.

"Good," he said. "I'll focus on the N.C. legislative officials and area members of Congress."

Annie immediately called Janet Pardel, the Asheville lawyer she'd interviewed who worked for the American Civil Liberties Union. Janet's reaction did not surprise her.

"We're just as shocked as everyone else," Janet said. "Fullspear was a mediocre lieutenant governor, but who's Rob Ryland? I'm suspicious of the Texas secession movement anyway. I know it has had a violent history and I'm sure he was an integral part of it."

"I guess the prudent thing is to keep a sharp eye on what he actually does," Annie said, trying to be neutral.

"I've heard that he and King Avery are lovers," Janet said. "Is that true?"

"I have no idea," Annie replied truthfully. She felt surprised that Janet had heard that rumor, despite hearing the same speculation herself. She didn't think Rob slept with men, given her regrettable history with him. On the other hand, what did she really know about Rob and his current activities?"

"Things will only get worse in this crazy new state," Janet said.

After a few more questions, responses and promises to follow up, Annie called Barbara Aydlette. The Gastonia woman had been watching TV, in between making calls to excited God's Gift members.

"Henry Fullspear was okay, I guess, but seemed to have a grumpy, grim personality when he spoke in public," Barbara said. "Apparently, this new guy is young and a real high-energy person who'll do anything to protect the interests of God's Gift Church and the new state. I can't wait to see what he and King will do."

"Oh, and Rob Ryland is so handsome," she said. "Between him and the gorgeous King Avery, I'll bet we have the best-looking leadership team of any church or state."

Barbara Aydlette's shallow comments disappointed Annie. She was afraid that a lot of church and Westcarolina officials would also judge Rob by his good looks and camera-ready comments. He had wisely kept a low profile so that most of Westcarolina was wondering, but knew little, about him.

The next step was going to be the hardest. Annie dialed Rob's office number to see what he'd say about his sudden elevation to the position of lieutenant governor.

"Who's this?" Rob demanded. He apparently didn't recognize her number.

"It's Annie Price," she said, trying to be as businesslike as possible.

"Oh, sweet Annie," he said, sounding happy, or perhaps just triumphant. "You're calling to congratulate me. Now that I'm lieutenant governor, you won't be able to resist me."

"Don't kid yourself, Rob. Besides, I hear you have a new lover named King."

He laughed. "Now that's just a baseless rumor. You know my heart belongs to you."

"This is wasting my time. What do you plan to do as lieutenant governor?"

"Whatever King wants me to do," he said in a more serious vein. "I can't say anything beyond the fact that there are big changes ahead."

"What about the Texas secessionists?" she asked. "Are you abandoning them? Aren't you still one of their big guys?"

"They have plenty of top leaders right now," Rob said. "I'd be a fool to let this opportunity go by. The secessionists are still trying to make Texas a new nation and are likely to struggle for a long time. The state of Westcarolina is a done deal, just ripe for change."

"I notice you haven't mentioned Henry Fullspear's accident," she said. "Don't you feel any sadness–or responsibility?"

"It wasn't my fault. You'd better not imply that I'm to blame. Henry wasn't being careful enough."

He thought for a minute before amending his statement.

"Change that to 'Henry Fullspear was a highly respected leader and longtime advocate for God's Gift Church. Given time, he would have been a great lieutenant governor.'

"That's what I want to say, and you'd better not write anything different," Rob said in a threatening voice.

After a few more questions that Rob answered with platitudes, she wound up the call.

"I have several deadlines to meet, Rob," she said. "If you have nothing more specific to tell me, I need to go."

"Darlin', you can call me anytime. I can see how it might work. I'll give you a good story and you'll give me a good time in bed. I'm counting on you to be extra nice to me."

Annie bristled and wondered why she let his obnoxious comments get to her. She needed to remain calm and to show him she was unruffled.

"Stop making those nasty comments. Don't even think about it."

CHAPTER 25

King and Rob were having their first planning meeting since Rob had become lieutenant governor a week earlier. Both were excited, knowing instinctively that they saw eye-to-eye on most plans to transform Westcarolina from a couple of dozen mountain counties into a unified Christian state.

Rob first brought up the vexing question of Wiccans. He said they were modern-day pagans who worshipped nature instead of God, sanctified the change of seasons, and espoused other blasphemous beliefs. They were essentially witches who were an affront to Westcarolina's reigning God's Gift Church.

"They should be stamped out," Rob said.

There were more than a hundred Wiccans living openly in the Asheville area, the seat of weird lifestyles, he said. There were at least a few dozen others scattered around the new state. It was hard to estimate, since Wiccans in smaller towns stayed quiet about their beliefs.

One coven had just announced a May Day ceremony in an Asheville city park. If previous rallies were any sign, it would be a bunch of unattractive, older women dancing around a stupid-looking maypole, Rob said.

"We need to do something. Since they're witches, maybe we should bring in a ducking stool and dunk them in the French Broad River. That would draw an enormous crowd and teach them a lesson."

"That wouldn't be acceptable," King said. "It's too weird to pass muster. After the plan to tax the churches failed, we need something different. My thought is that we give them a chance to join a God's

Gift congregation. If they won't do that, pay them a stipend–maybe $2,000 each–to move out of Westcarolina."

"Now you're talking," Rob said. "That's brilliant, but would $2,000 each be enough?"

"I'm trying to think what the church could comfortably afford. Some Wiccans would be happy with it and others would want more. Some would rather join the church."

King announced his plan Sunday from one of his Gastonia churches, which was beamed to all God's Gift congregations. The church members met the proposal with clapping, whistling and shouts of agreement.

Annie and Jim, who routinely watched the broadcasts of King's services, felt appalled. They'd heard that Wiccans might be the next to feel King's iron glove, but to force them to move out of Westcarolina was cruel–and blatantly illegal.

Annie quickly called Janet Pardel, her source who was a lawyer for the ACLU.

"We're on it," Janet said. "We're suing tomorrow morning on behalf of Janna Pickering and five other members of an Asheville coven, their primary political and social organization."

"Any way to talk to Ms. Pickering for our story?" Annie asked.

"Sure, here's the number."

When Annie got Pickering on the phone, it was obvious that the woman had been crying. She said she'd become a Wiccan in college and continued to follow its philosophy. At 36, her best friends were older and longtime Wiccans.

"It's just a different way of seeing the world," she said. "I believe in nature–the sun, the moon, and all sources of light that make our lives worth living. There is nothing evil in my life; I try to be a good neighbor and friend.

"I don't want to join God's Gift Church and I definitely don't want to move. Asheville is my home. My job as a computer programmer is here and all my relatives."

Janna sobbed as Annie interviewed her. She promised to keep in touch.

Next, Annie called Barnard Siff, a newly installed God's Gift minister in the westernmost mountain town of Murphy. She needed an opposing point of view.

"I don't always agree with King Avery, but I think he's on target about the Wiccans," Siff said. "I don't like the thought of them teaching our young children or having positions of authority that might contaminate our glorious new state."

"Isn't kicking them out against the law? Discrimination based on religion or creed?" Annie said.

"It sounds eminently practical to me. The Wiccans get paid to move, so they're getting an excellent incentive."

The next day, a federal judge issued a restraining order against the God's Gift plan to force Wiccans to join the church or leave the state. The full case probably wouldn't be heard for months.

Annie called King Avery to ask him what he thought about the judge's ruling. King was philosophical.

"We knew we were taking a chance, but the Wiccans are a blot on the state. We hoped a judge would agree."

"A lot of people have called to say they think your proposal is shocking. What have Wiccans done to hurt anyone or anything in Westcarolina?"

She hoped to goad King into saying something outrageous that would reveal more of his true feelings. He didn't.

"Annie, you listen too much to liberal viewpoints," King said. "But we can discuss that some other time. You'll have to come to the mountain or Gastonia for lunch. I believe in what you do as a reporter. I just think you're wrong about this."

Late in the afternoon, Annie watched the TV news station covering the Asheville coven's May Day celebration. She saw a dozen mostly middle-aged women in long, sheer dresses dancing around a maypole, looking a bit silly. Annie saw a younger woman she thought might be Janna, the Wiccan she'd talked to on the phone. That woman was wearing a rainbow-colored dress and looked happy to be with her friends.

"What's the harm in Wiccans?" Jake asked. He was home and had come into the living room to watch the May Day celebration with her. He said he'd seen similar demonstrations in Austin, which had a much-quoted motto, "Keep Austin weird."

Annie was glad that Jake was tolerant of different lifestyles. If he'd been narrow-minded, like members of God's Gift Church she'd talked to, she didn't think she'd be able to live with him.

As she watched the Asheville TV report, the sudden appearance of about 100 demonstrators caught her attention. Many identified themselves as members of God's Gift Church on their placards. Homemade slogans said, "Blasphemy: Witches move out!" and "God's word: Wiccans don't believe it."

She watched in horror as the demonstrators, a few with baseball bats swinging, surrounded the dozen or so Wiccans, who looked nervous, but continued to dance and sing.

Police in riot gear arrived quickly and dispersed the crowd. The church members and others complied but seemed disappointed; the small group of Wiccans looked relieved.

Annie and Jim revised their story for the next day, focusing on how the rally had brought both sides out in what could have been a violent confrontation. Among others, they quoted King, and the ACLU's Janet.

Satisfied that the long story represented opposing views, the rally and the court action, they filed it for the website and the next day's paper. The Associated Press picked it up and the story drew an international audience. Annie and Jim were besieged with calls from subscribers and many reporters, including one from the *New York Times*.

At the Blowing Rock office, King and Rob privately expressed their disappointment with Annie and Jim's story and the court decision. Rob was especially critical.

"Annie's got to go, one way or another," he said. "She and her younger sidekick are going to mess up everything we try to do. Her byline is always listed at the top of every story. If she were gone, young Jim would fall in line."

"Not going to happen," King said. "We'll just work harder to get our viewpoint across. I think we can handle this."

CHAPTER 26

An uneasy peace had prevailed in the Price-Satterfield household since the night of the party. Annie had resolved not to be jealous of Jake's flirtatiousness and Jake was being especially solicitous of Annie's condition.

Tonight, however, Jake wasn't his normal self, cracking jokes that left Annie laughing helplessly and paying extra attention to her tales of reporting that day. He was quiet and seemed absorbed in his own thoughts.

He'd fixed a nice baked chicken dinner for them and watched closely to make sure she ate her green beans and salad. Annie thought how lucky she was to have a husband who cooked decent meals and kept the house somewhat orderly. Between work and home, her pregnancy had left her with little energy and time for household tasks and cooking.

"Annie, I need to talk to you. Let's sit on the sofa so you can be comfortable."

Annie froze. Was he going to tell her something dire, perhaps that he was going back to Texas, or didn't want to be married any longer? She looked at his face and he had no trace of a smile.

"You know that secret project I've been working on for the last few months?" he asked.

"Yeah. Can you tell me about it now?"

"I'm getting ahead of myself by a few hours, but I believe it's important for you to know that the Garnett Corp. will make an announcement tomorrow about buying the *Charlotte Press*. I've been the chief lawyer for Garnett for months."

Annie was relieved that Jake's news had nothing to do with their relationship. But she also felt sick to her stomach. The idea of Jake representing Garnett was repugnant. The large newspaper company was renowned for its cheapness in reporter salaries and projects. Its top leaders of their papers also seemed heartless about laying off reporters.

"Jake, how could you?" she said. "Garnett is about the worst company around. All it does is cut, cut, cut. I may be out of a job soon."

"I doubt it. Garnett knows the new state requires more and deeper reporting. Besides, just between us, it was the only media company that made a bid. The family is frantic to sell the paper and get its money to split between the heirs."

"When I came to work in Charlotte, the editors were so sure that we were on an upward path," she said. "I'm not sure I would have taken the job if I'd known the newspaper would be for sale so quickly. I was looking for stability."

"A lot can change in a few months," Jake said. "For a while, it looked as though there was interest in running it from one of the younger family members. But he changed his mind. Families don't think newspapers are the sure bet that they used to be. The Carters see the paper as a millstone around their necks, preventing them from doing other things with their lives."

Annie tried to digest the upsetting news. What did her future hold? How would her colleagues in the newsroom react to the fact that Jake had brokered the deal? Would she be seen as an accomplice to destroying the paper?

"I hope you didn't move here just to work on this deal," she said, annoyed that she'd known nothing about it.

"Annie, that's unworthy of you," Jake said, looking angry. "I moved here to marry you and create a family with our little girl."

They had recently found out that the child Annie was carrying was a healthy girl. Both were ecstatic. Annie wouldn't admit it, but she'd really wanted a girl. She thought a girl would be more fun and easier to raise, but Jake assured her that wasn't true. He pointed out that his girls were entirely different from each other and that each was a challenge in different ways.

"Does Garnett know that you have a wife who works at the *Press?*"

"Yeah," he said. "Whoever becomes the publisher won't treat you any different from any other staff member. The Garnett team just asked that I operate under complete secrecy. That's why I waited till tonight to say anything to you. I trust you won't tell anyone before tomorrow's meeting."

"Of course not. Will you be there tomorrow?" she asked, more curious than angry now.

"Yeah. I'll be part of the meeting, though I don't particularly want to."

The next morning, a newsroom message went out announcing a mandatory 10 a.m. meeting. The gossip was already circulating that it involved the sale of the paper.

Reporters and editors gathered as usual at the front of the newsroom as 10 a.m. approached. The slight, balding figure of publisher Fordham Carter III was waiting there. He motioned for quiet as he prepared to speak.

"Folks, as some of you know, I've always been the biggest proponent for local ownership of newspapers. The Carter family has owned the *Press* for over ninety years and there's always been a Carter or other family member at the helm. Unfortunately, we've run out of Carters who want to take on this responsibility. We decided that the time had come to sell."

Everyone was quiet, digesting the news.

"I want to introduce the lawyer who's been an integral part of working with the paper and finding a prospective owner, Jake Satterfield."

Jake, wearing his best navy suit and accompanied by a tall man in a gray suit and wire-rimmed spectacles, strode to the front of the room. As some staff members, including those who'd been at the recent staff party, recognized Jake, there was some murmuring. He introduced himself and the man beside him.

"This is Hank Sisson, chairman of the Garnett Corp.," Jake said. "He's thrilled to be part of the new ownership of this paper and wants it to be the flagship of the company. I know you'll have some questions for him."

Annie's partner, Jim, asked the question on everyone's mind.

"Will the print edition stay, or will you go all digital, as a lot of papers have done?"

"We will definitely keep the print edition and hire a few more reporters to cover areas where we're weakest; writing more about the arts, coverage of minority concerns and putting more emphasis on the new state of Westcarolina," Sisson said. "As long as the print edition earns its way—and it's doing all right—things will stay the way they are. Of course, we'll keep trying to upgrade the digital product, as all papers are doing."

Jim, president of the recently formed newsroom union, had apparently been designated to ask all the questions. He got straightforward answers: no layoffs or buyouts for the foreseeable future, no attempts to weaken the union, yearly raises, and small increases in vacation time for those who'd been there the longest.

"We will reassess the financial situation after a year, and these policies will continue to be in effect until then," said Sisson.

Only Annie knew, according to their conversation the previous night, how much Jake had pushed for those policies. He'd designed a contract with many of those promises in writing. Annie was proud of him and hoped that when reporters asked her the inevitable questions, she could do justice to his role. However, she felt awkward about admitting her ignorance of his work with Garnett for so long. But she knew that some would understand the need for the company's secrecy.

"And now, I want to introduce you to the first Garnett publisher for the *Press*," said Sisson. "Someone you're already familiar with—managing editor Amanda Weeks."

Amanda smiled at the widespread applause. She was well-liked in the newsroom and looked happy. Annie hoped her new job would allay some fears about Garnett.

"I second the information that Hank provided to Jim," she said. "We're already good and with a few more resources, we'll be the best newspaper in the South."

The staffers left the meeting cautiously, surprised by the preponderance of good news. It seemed the opposite of what the reporters and editors were hearing at other newspapers. But could they believe it? Annie, like most of the reporters in the room, was skeptical–not of Jake, but of the new owners. Her training as an investigative reporter told her not to listen to the words, but to weigh the results.

Jim said it best. "We're doing pretty well, and they say they want to put money into what they see as their flagship newspaper. Now if they'll only keep their word."

CHAPTER 27

Claire Avery swooped into King's office, wearing white designer jeans with a silk gray top and silver sandals. She looked absolutely smashing, as usual, but her husband was immune to her charms.

"I've got the party plans, including the list of people to be invited," she said. "Of course, you'll probably want to add to what I'm giving you."

"Yeah, and I want this party to reflect more of the church's values than the last two," King said. "The annual get-together is getting a poor reputation, and we can't afford that in a new state."

Claire looked disappointed.

"You're just becoming an old fuddy-duddy. If God's Gift's top members and supporters of Westcarolina can't let down their hair once a year, there will be some grumbling. It's already bad enough that we're only serving beer and soft drinks."

"You know that's going to be the new policy," King said. "I wanted to ban selling all alcohol in this state, but a few top church members have persuaded me otherwise. They say that selling beer in the new state–without wine, liquor and ABC stores–is a good compromise between going wide open and going dry.

"Things I don't want at the party: anybody getting visibly drunk, using drugs, openly taking someone's spouse to one of the bedrooms or getting loud and obnoxious," King added. "I'm going to invite a few reporters and a bunch of legislators, and I want them to experience just a nice summer party."

"Do you think it's smart to invite reporters?" Claire asked. "Won't that just give them more ammunition to write negative stories?"

"I think that will stop them from continually asking about the party, for one thing. It seems to overshadow a lot of things the church is doing well."

"Well, I'm going to do whatever I want to."

"You know, I don't care who you take as a lover, as long as you're discreet. I don't know why you do this. I've asked you repeatedly if you want a divorce and you've said no every time."

"The church can't do without me and my daddy's money. You shouldn't forget that. I'm content with the status quo and you should be, too. Besides, remember how much fun we had last year when you watched?"

Claire had read lots of stories about the sexual shenanigans of Jerry Falwell Jr., his wife, and the Florida pool boy. She had persuaded King to do the same thing that Falwell allegedly did–to sit in a corner watching while Claire and last year's lover had sex.

"You know I didn't have fun. I only did it once for you, and I'll never do it again. To be honest, it made me sick. Do you want us to lose everything we've worked for?"

"No, but I don't want to pass up chances for a relationship that could be fun and add some purpose to my boring life."

"Claire, what's wrong with you? I give you everything you want. I try my best to please you and don't make demands on you to be a woman's leader in the church."

"You'd better not," she said. "You know I don't really believe in all that claptrap you preach."

"Once again, are you sure you don't want to at least try a separation?" She shook her head. He knew she enjoyed the prestige of marriage to a well-known evangelistic minister.

Reading between the lines, King surmised that her last lover, the software mogul, had dumped Claire, and she was eager to prove her desirability once again.

He spent some time looking at Claire's party planning lists. She'd gone all out this year with decorations and food. She was no fool.

Claire knew the party had to showcase the best of God's Gift Church and the growing professional staff of Westcarolina.

Claire was a terrible wife, but he had to give her credit for party planning. He wished she could do it full time rather than chasing after men. He didn't know quite what was wrong with her but suspected her rich and indulgent daddy had spoiled her for a normal life.

Well, he didn't have the time or energy to analyze Claire. He had to think straight before the invitations went out. Was he doing the right thing by inviting Annie, her husband, and Jim, her reporting partner? Invitations would also go to several upper-level executives at the Charlotte paper, including Amanda Weeks, the new publisher.

He knew he couldn't resist inviting Annie and wanted to meet her husband. He increasingly thought about her and wished he could see her more often. In fact, he invented reasons for her to come by the Charlotte or Gastonia offices and interview him.

Rob saw it and teased him about his "crush," but King witnessed the two of them together and concluded that Rob was also besotted with the reporter in his own rough fashion. He'd heard Rob teasing Annie in a sexual way and had asked him privately to stop.

"Boy, do you have it bad," Rob laughed. "Annie's tough as nails. She can take whatever you throw at her."

King changed the subject quickly, because he also admired Rob for many reasons, among them his lean, sexy body and angelic face. He watched for signs that Rob returned his admiration, but so far, hadn't seen any. King wasn't bisexual or secretly gay. That didn't mean he couldn't appreciate a handsome man.

He went through the list again and added a few more newspaper people from Asheville and other larger towns in Westcarolina. He didn't want to appear that he was playing favorites with the Charlotte reporters.

He wondered how the invitation would be received. Mostly, he hoped Annie would come.

CHAPTER 28

Large, embossed envelopes addressed to Jim and Annie came in the newsroom mail in early June. Since she rarely got anything but press releases and junk mail, which were often the same, she ripped into hers with curiosity.

It was an invitation from King and Claire Avery to the annual party at their mountain home. Annie had teased King about the party, daring him to invite her. She'd heard that the event included drug use, illicit sex in the upstairs bedrooms and heavy drinking. King had said it was hard to monitor the behavior of several hundred people, but he'd assured her he'd tried to make the event squeaky clean.

She called to accept the invitation and got King himself.

"I'm thrilled that you're coming and look forward to meeting your husband. I think you'll find that the party is much tamer than its reputation."

"Oh, don't tell me that," Annie said, laughing. "Of course, Jake will look forward to it. He works at home and is always thinking of ways to go out."

She, Jim and several of the top-level editors who were also invited, had decided that the social occasion probably didn't merit coverage unless something unusual happened. King had noted that the church's social fund paid for the event's expenditures. She'd done some checking and found that was true.

Annie was in a quandary about what to wear. She thought her pregnant figure looked so large it would be difficult to fit. After putting it off till the day before the party, she went shopping at a high-end store. She tried on at least ten dressy maternity outfits before ending up with a long, sparkly dark green dress with spaghetti straps and a bodice that showed off her increasingly full breasts.

The next day, Jake drove them to their Blowing Rock hotel in the late afternoon. She thought it would be better to dress there than sit in the car for two hours, wrinkle her dress and spoil her makeup. When they got to the hotel, she took a long, luxurious shower and liberally applied her favorite floral perfume and more makeup than usual. She put on dangly silver and diamond earrings that Jake had given her and silver sandals with a low heel. Did she need pearls? She tried on a strand, but decided they looked too matronly with her outfit.

She worried that perhaps her dress was too daring, but for once in her pregnancy, she wanted to ditch her modest outfits and really shine. After she'd finished dressing, she walked into the living room of the suite. Jake, who'd already dressed and was reading legal papers, looked up. She walked down an imaginary runway and twirled in the fancy dress. He couldn't take his eyes off her.

"I'm really lucky to be squiring the most beautiful woman in Charlotte and Westcarolina," he said after a wolf whistle.

"Even with my pregnancy?"

"Babe, you look so luscious, I'm tempted to skip the party and have our own private evening."

When they arrived, the mansion looked gorgeous. The party planners had removed all the furniture from the large living area and replaced it with decorated tables. One corner featured a podium and a small dance floor. In the adjoining dining room, caterers rushed in and out, setting up stations of food. The large deck was lit with sparkling lights and featured a glowing fire pit. People were already milling around, talking and drinking.

There was a short receiving line with King, Rob and a few Westcarolina government officials. King's eyes lit up when he saw her, and he welcomed Jake warmly as well.

"Annie, you look stunning," King said. "None of God's creations is more beautiful than a pregnant woman."

Rob, for once, was decent to her, making no sexual remarks. Of course, he'd probably been told to be on his best behavior.

"Well done, Price," he said after staring at her breasts. "Great dress."

Jake was simmering as they walked away. "That guy has incredible nerve checking you out like that, after what he did to you."

Annie, who'd told Jake about Rob's past behavior, said, "Let it go. He'd love it if you made a scene. What he doesn't like is to be ignored. So, we'll just ignore him the rest of the evening. This is a party, and we should enjoy it."

They found the large table with other newspaper people from Charlotte and Westcarolina. She chatted with Jim and his wife Naomi while Jake went to the bar to get a non-alcoholic drink for her and bourbon for himself. He came back with sparkling water and a beer.

"With a fancy party like this, you'd think they'd have something better than cheap beer," he complained.

"King Avery has said in the past that Westcarolina was going to be dry," Annie said, thinking hard. "He must have changed his mind."

She looked at the beer bottle and noticed it was a local brand brewed in West Jefferson, a scenic mountain town about 30 miles from Blowing Rock. Her intuition was telling her there was something suspicious about that. She told him to take cellphone pictures of all the beer labels. She'd check it out later.

They hit the buffet, which offered stations of succulent meats, seafood and pasta, crowned with a long table of desserts. The desserts looked deliciously homemade, and Annie wondered if God's Gift church ladies had stepped in. She asked, and the caterer said those with "special talents" had offered their services. Annie nearly swooned when she tasted a slice of butterscotch pie.

"I wish I'd skipped all the healthy stuff and just had desserts," she said to Jake.

"That's my girl," he said with a laugh. "That baby of ours is going to be a sugar fanatic."

"You may be right. But you cook me a healthy dinner almost every night. I'm sure she gets everything she needs."

Annie looked for King as they finished their desserts. She thought he must be worn out after greeting what she estimated was about 150 guests. He stood on a specially constructed stage in the corner of the cavernous room and spoke easily to the crowd.

"Welcome to Westcarolina," he said. "We're a blend of the New South and the Wild West. Just kidding. We hope to be anything but wild. Now, introduce yourself to some of the finest people in the world–Westcarolinians–and enjoy the music."

Besides Jake, who wore a traditional dinner jacket with his usual aplomb, King was the handsomest man there, she thought. His tux looked new, dark blue and tailored to show off his slim, muscled figure. He caught her appreciative gaze and winked. She looked away, embarrassed to be caught staring.

Annie wandered to the restroom, combed her long, curled hair and freshened her makeup. When she returned, Jake was talking animatedly with Claire Avery, who'd taken Annie's seat at the table. She looked spectacular in a gold-spangled sheath dress with matching stilettos. Claire got up and chatted briefly with Annie before smiling at Jake and walking away.

Jake whispered to Annie after she'd disappeared into the crowd. "Are you sure she's the pastor's wife? She just propositioned me– invited me to a 'quiet suite upstairs to get to know me.' As you know, sweetie, I'm no prude, but that was over the top."

"I've heard that she does that to someone at every party, despite her position as the pastor's wife," Annie whispered back. "She must think you're as handsome as I do."

The band struck up soft rock music and Annie saw King Avery heading their way. After talking with them and others at the table, he bowed to Annie.

"Could I have the next dance, beautiful lady?"

Annie looked at Jake, who said, "Go on, sweetheart. You should dance while you still can."

The band played "Unchained Melody," the romantic oldie first sung by the Righteous Brothers. King put his arms around her expanded waist and held her more tightly than she had expected. She hesitantly rested her hands lightly on his broad shoulders, pulling back a little. They chatted easily for a minute or two, then he just looked at her with his startling blue eyes.

Annie realized that his feelings for her were getting too complicated. Although she increasingly liked him, she would not fall into the trap of any kind of relationship. She was married now, and though they'd had their differences, she loved Jake passionately. Still, a handsome man's admiration for her in her condition felt flattering.

King brought her back to the table, chatted for a few minutes with the other journalists and said with apparent regret he'd have to get back to table-hopping. Like most politicians, he'd made everyone feel good before he left.

"Enjoy, my journalist friends, and if you need anything, don't hesitate to call me directly."

"I didn't like the way he was holding you and staring," Jake whispered after King had stopped at another table. A few of the other journalists were talking softly, possibly about her and King. Jake glared in the governor's direction.

"I know, I know," she said. "This party has worn me out and I'm ready to call it a night. Are there any beers you didn't try?"

"No, I sampled all four. Each was worse than the last," he said in a low voice.

They made their goodbyes to Claire since King was deep in conversation across the room and retrieved their car for the drive to the nearby hotel. Annie was pleasant, but cool to Claire.

"That was one of the damnedest parties I've ever been to," Jake said, bemused. "The pastor who's the host manhandles a pregnant reporter on the dance floor, and the pastor's wife tries to lure the reporter's husband to a bedroom. Are you sure these folks lead a church?

"Incredible."

CHAPTER 29

A couple of days after King's party, Annie started making inquiries about beer, wine and Alcoholic Beverage Control liquors in Westcarolina.

King had caught her off-guard when he announced on TV during Sunday's sermon that beer sales would be allowed in the new state, but that liquor and wine retailing would be banned. She'd listened to some of his sermons from the last few years and noticed that the evils of alcohol were hardly mentioned.

Annie thought his stance was inconsistent, to say the least. If beer was permitted, she thought all kinds of alcohol should be legal. She had a hunch that she wanted to follow.

Armed with cellphone pictures of four beer bottles that Jake had taken, she decided to visit at least two of the large Westcarolina breweries near Charlotte that distributed their beer, rather than just selling it onsite. There were at least 40 good-sized breweries/distributors in Westcarolina, mostly in tourist-oriented areas, such as Asheville and Blowing Rock, she found from research.

A few counties in the far western reaches of Westcarolina had been "dry" until the last few years, that is, they allowed no sales of alcohol. Annie was surprised to discover that all Westcarolina counties now permitted the sale of beer.

It was a beautiful July day when she drove west toward the mountains. Annie was so glad to get out of the office. Since she'd become pregnant, especially early on when she was battling morning sickness, she had done most of her interviews by phone.

There was nothing like being on the road, especially for brief trips that showed her more of the new state she was covering. She drove west of uptown, appreciating the sight of planes taking off and heading toward landing at nearby Charlotte/Douglas International Airport. She exited onto U.S. 74, enjoying the luxuriant poplars, pines, oaks and other tall trees lining the highway. North Carolina had so many more trees across the state highways than Texas. West Texas and so many parts of the Lone Star State were nearly devoid of trees.

Her destination was Shelby, a city of about 20,000 that had a brewery she wanted to see. She'd heard that Shelby was picturesque, interesting, and only about 40 miles from Charlotte. There was also a regionally renowned restaurant she wanted to try, Bridges Barbecue Lodge, so she looked for it along the commercial stretch of highway toward downtown Shelby.

Annie spotted the humble-looking barbecue place by the large number of cars clustered around it. She could tell that the owners had added a wing onto the original modest building, presumably to accommodate more diners. She walked inside the dark paneled restaurant and found a seat at the bar just before a flock of diners lined up inside the door. A mixture of Black men, White men and a few women of both races were convivial as they waited either for a table or a takeout order.

Annie ordered the pork barbecue with hush puppies and potato salad. The food was brought quickly, and she savored the warm meat with the spicy sauce. There was only one dessert, banana pudding, and she ordered it, calories be damned. It looked entirely homemade, without the store-bought pudding that most restaurants used. As she surveyed the large bowl with whipped cream, she wished Jake was there to eat half. Of course, she ate it all anyway, rationalizing that her pregnancy required large infusions of food.

She drove into Shelby, impressed by the tree-lined streets with small businesses around the courthouse square. She noticed that what she guessed was the former Cleveland County courthouse was now the Earl Scruggs Center–Music and Stories from the American South. She knew that Scruggs, the famous banjo player and composer, was a Shelby native. She'd make a special trip back soon to go to the museum.

She found the brewery/distributor she'd been looking for on the outskirts of town. Jake had saved a bottle from the party with the label named Salvo. The long, low brick building looked like it had once been a cotton manufacturer. Salvo Brewery also offered food and outdoor picnic-table seating in the back of the structure, according to an advertising sheet she picked up at the door.

She quickly found Bob Barrett, manager of the brewery and distributor of Salvo. Bob, balding and overweight around the middle (from a regular sampling of his product, no doubt) was eager to talk about the beer, which had a regular and a light version. He said it was available in most Westcarolina stores. He was hoping for national distribution in the next few years.

Annie said her husband Jake had tried the beer at King Avery's big party over the weekend.

"What did he think of Salvo?" Bob asked in an excited voice.

Annie hesitated. She didn't want to hurt his feelings or make an enemy of this well-meaning man.

"Jake said it was especially tasty with orange slices. Where did you get the name Salvo?"

"Don't you know? God's Gift Church owns it," Bob said. "Salvo is short for salvation. It's enormously popular so far in Westcarolina."

Since it was still early, she decided to drive on to Hickory, another city in Westcarolina close to Charlotte.

She met Phil Paton, CEO and manager of a mid-sized brewery a few miles from Hickory's center. The Sun Brewery sold and distributed its signature brand called Sun, short for Sunday and a reference to the Son of God, Phil said. He was cordial, but not as loquacious as Bob Barrett. Annie, noticing that he was thin, thought he probably didn't enjoy beer as much.

She'd located the brewery right away. The low-slung building with a modern design looked new. From the parking lot, she could see the brewing equipment through floor to ceiling windows. The place had plenty of tables and chairs and, he boasted, an excellent chef who prepared traditional Carolina and southern foods. Even if its customers didn't like beer, they could enjoy a night out with good food.

It was much the same story. God's Gift owns Sun Brewery Phil said. Ninety percent of the ownership and profits would go to Westcarolina. The church would keep the remaining ten percent.

"My husband and I noticed it was a big hit at King Avery's recent party at his Blowing Rock house," Annie said.

"I'm prejudiced, of course, but I think it's the best beer that God's Gift Church produces," Phil said. "Come with me, and I'll show you the brewery and production equipment. I'll even give you a case of beer to take home."

"Since I'm pregnant, I can't drink alcohol," Annie said. "The newspaper wouldn't allow me to accept such an expensive gift, anyway. But I'd love to see your facility."

Phil also showed her three party rooms, from small to large, where area residents held everything from bridal showers to retirement parties. The Sun brewery was clearly a social center in the medium-sized city.

When she got back to the office, Annie made phone calls to as many of the brewery/distributors in Westcarolina that she could identify. What she found didn't surprise her. She learned that, besides the two that she had visited, God's Gift Church owned thirteen others, most of which were recent acquisitions. The mega-church operated all those breweries as side businesses, and soon they would transfer 90 percent of the ownership to the state government.

The next step was to look at wine purveyors. Then she'd call King and get his explanation.

CHAPTER 30

Annie decided she'd visit several wine stores she'd noticed on her drive to the breweries the day before. She wanted plenty of ammunition before she interviewed King.

The first store, on the outskirts of Morganton, a small city near Hickory, was called Fine Wines for Less. It was in a large brick building that looked like it had been around for a while. Information she'd found online showed the same ownership for over ten years.

It was early afternoon, well past the lunch hour, and the store had few customers. When she identified herself and asked to see the manager, a middle-aged man came out of what appeared to be a storage area.

She could see several red wine stains on his plaid shirt, and he was sweating, probably from lifting boxes full of bottles of wine. He introduced himself as Ted Byrum.

Annie asked if he'd heard that beer would be the only alcoholic product sold in the new state. She told him that people attending King's recent party were disappointed that no wine or liquor was served.

"Yeah, it's easier for God's Gift church to dominate the beer distribution business. Wine retailers would be harder, because they mostly consist of a few national chains that aren't going to sell to a church."

Annie asked him if he knew that God's Gift Church had bought at least 15 breweries/distributors in Westcarolina and that it would keep 10 percent of the ownership.

"I didn't know for sure, but I suspected it," he said. "There are plenty of people who like beer, but other drinkers prefer wine or a cocktail. King Avery seems to drink only beer, from what I've heard. Maybe that's why he's allowing it, but no liquor or wine sales."

Annie said she'd asked for a list from the state of North Carolina showing ownership of all the breweries and wine retailing outlets. Westcarolina records were still incomplete.

A newer, national chain called Wines of the World beckoned in Hickory. It was in a busy strip shopping center with supermarket carts lined up outside.

Inside, a half-dozen shoppers had carts partially filled with wines, including some varieties and vintages that Annie recognized as pricey. A fortyish woman neatly dressed in a navy pants outfit came up to Annie and introduced herself as Martha Bowen, store manager. She asked Annie how she could help.

Annie, as usual, identified herself as a *Press* reporter and explained why she was there.

"My boss asked me what was going on and I told him--that only beer could be sold in the new state and that God's Gift Church owned close to half of the breweries that distribute their products," Bowen said.

"That's right. There's a small share of profits for the church and probably will include money for the businesspeople who helped to buy them," Annie said. "What Gov. Avery has said publicly is that beer is less harmful to drinkers than liquor, but there's no basis for that view."

"Many of our customers drink nothing but wine," she said. "They often have just a glass with a fine meal, but I'm sure that many drink to excess. Since we're part of a national chain, God's Gift church couldn't afford to buy us. Is he trying to legislate morality? It didn't work with Prohibition, and it won't work here."

"He's said that this will be a state governed by God's Gift beliefs and practices, but everyone who lives here is not a member of that church, or any church," said Annie.

"Yeah, the church is so pervasive in this new state that I'm afraid it will drive people back to North Carolina," Bowen said.

For the last interview of her trip, Annie visited a small wine shop she'd noticed in the Westcarolina capital of Gastonia. Porter's Wines was on an unassuming downtown street and consisted of one medium-sized room with a stock area in the back.

A thin man with wire-rimmed glasses who looked about 60 greeted her with a friendly hello. He introduced himself as Frank Porter and said he'd owned the small business for twenty years. It specialized in hard-to-find European wines.

Since most wine businesses were boutique low-profit retailers or superstores, the church probably control Westcarolina wine sales, he noted.

"It can't monopolize the wine business. Most are multi-store chains that would be beyond the capabilities of God's Gift to acquire. The church is putting its resources into the brewery businesses."

"What will you do?"

"I thought about moving to Charlotte and setting up a small shop there," he said. "But honestly, I'm ready to retire and stores selling boutique wines aren't that popular anymore."

She got back to the office and called some ABC stores in Westcarolina. Managers were less apt to talk, because North Carolina operated the stores under a temporary contract with the new state. They were merely paid staff. But a few said Gov. Avery was just trying to squelch competition for the church-owned breweries by closing ABC stores.

Annie talked with her editor and decided now was the time to interview King about the issue. She found out that he was at his Charlotte office for the day and welcomed a chance to walk the few blocks to it.

It was a beautiful day for a stroll in uptown Charlotte. It was still warm, but there was a sense of fall in the air. Annie looked forward to questioning King Avery.

CHAPTER 31

King's secretary buzzed him, as he was trying to decide on several candidates to lead a Westcarolina department. Staffing a new state government from the ground up was getting to be too much for him, and he'd have to hire more people just to assist him with hiring more people. His lieutenant governor, Rob Ryland, was of course a great help, but sometimes he didn't entirely trust Rob's judgment. He was awfully cynical, while King still believed in the basic decency of people. King supposed that was the difference between being a revolutionary fighter and a man of the cloth.

He put aside the resumes when his secretary told him Annie Price was there to ask some questions. He quickly called in Rob and asked what Annie wanted. Rob followed Annie's every move assiduously.

"I suspect she wants to talk to you about our breweries," Rob said. "I've heard she's been nosing around them."

"I'll handle her," King said, reflecting on the strange animosity between Annie and Rob. "You can listen in on the system."

Annie walked in wearing one of her signature black maternity outfits. He guessed she had walked over from the paper because her cheeks were rosy, and he could smell her perfume mixed with perspiration. To King, she looked beautiful. He hadn't seen her since his party, where, according to his wife, he'd held her much too tightly on the dance floor.

"Hi, Annie. What can I do for you?"

"I wanted to ask you about your new policy on banning liquor and wine sales and permitting only beer sales in Westcarolina."

"Well, I'll explain it, but it's complicated. I wanted to ban all alcohol businesses, but my people advised allowing beer so that casual drinkers would have an option."

"Why do you think liquor and wine sales should be banned?"

"Liquor products and sometimes wine cause more damage and heartache than most any legal substances," King said. "I've seen it time and time again in my ministry. Beer causes fewer problems because it's more filling and people generally drink less."

"Do you have any studies that show such a thing? I don't think so. People who want to get drunk will get drunk on any kind of alcohol. They will drink as much as it takes, whether it's beer, wine or liquor."

Annie paused before going to the heart of her questions.

"Could it be that your administration wants to keep the beer business legal because God's Gift Church owns fifteen breweries in Westcarolina? I'm talking about breweries that distribute their money-making products all over the new state and are expanding into surrounding states."

King, looking sheepish, said, "God's Gift Church is the beating heart of the state. Anything we can do to advance it, we'll do. We predict that within two years, nine out of ten residents will belong to a God's Gift congregation."

"But aren't you jeopardizing God's Gift's tax-exempt status by buying these businesses?"

King took his time before answering.

"We plan to transfer 90 percent of each business to Westcarolina's government," he said. "The church will keep 10 percent, sort of like tithing. We also need to share the profits with our benefactors. The purchases were made through God's Gift because we have many church supporters who are generous with their assets.

"We don't think it's illegal, because it's clearly established that churches and governments can own property, but we'll let the courts decide," he said. "Also, we have notified the state of North Carolina that we won't be part of their ABC system. That state understands that we want to make our own alcohol laws. Have you ever seen

North Carolina's ABC warehouse in Raleigh? It's acres long and pernicious to all Christian people.

"The ABC business is not as profitable as owning our own products," he said. "The breweries that distribute will keep on giving as their products become more popular across the Carolinas and beyond."

King, despite his warm feelings for Annie, was getting angry with her as she questioned him.

"Is that all, Annie? I'm very busy and it's getting late in the day. I'm sure you have a deadline for another one of your unfair stories."

"This story will be fair," she said. "If you have problems with it, you can call me tomorrow." She got up from her chair nearest his desk and left, head held high.

Rob came in the side door from the listening room, where he was eavesdropping eagerly.

"I thought you handled her pretty well," he said. "You gave her answers for everything. And I suspect that big wine and liquor businesses will sue us, sooner rather than later. Be prepared for some conflict and ugliness, though I know you don't like that."

CHAPTER 32

As predicted, a few large liquor distributors and some national wine retailers doing business in Westcarolina promptly sued the state and God's Gift Church over its new policy. A judge issued a restraining order on any further purchases of breweries while the case was pending. Some officials in the N.C. legislature criticized the Westcarolina plan to close ABC stores, saying it would encourage smuggling and ramp up the illegal production and sale of moonshine. Moonshine was historically popular in parts of the mountains.

King, stung by the negative reaction, especially in some tourist areas of Westcarolina, used his Sunday broadcast from one of God's Gift churches in Gastonia to defend his actions.

"As you know, many followers of God's Gift Church don't drink alcohol. Others, like me, indulge in a beer on occasion. In the past, I preached total abstinence, but my view has evolved. Many people relax with a beer after work, then go about their business. The danger is to sit around drinking all night. That tendency is more prevalent with the consumption of liquor and wine. That's why the church strongly advises against it," he said.

"Some people have asked me if I have studies that prove beer is more benign than other forms of alcohol. I don't, but I have a lot of practical knowledge with the counseling I do."

Annie and Jim had gone to the church after hearing King would make a speech about his latest initiative. They looked at each other and Jim shook his head slightly, confident that churchgoers would see the hypocrisy of King's past support for abstinence and the fallacies of his argument for selling beer only.

"To take advantage of a booming industry and help our new state's economy, the church has bought fifteen breweries in Westcarolina and plans to buy more," King said.

"The breweries aren't just popular gathering places–they all sell and distribute their products in our new state and beyond. The government of Westcarolina will receive 90 percent of the assets of each business. Ten percent will remain the property of God's Gift Church, and there are legal ways to make sure that happens. We've already consulted a lawyer about it."

"As God's Gift deeds 90 percent of the ownership of the breweries to the state of Westcarolina, profits from the acquisitions will go to improve Westcarolina roads and bridges. We'll also be providing extra support to public education," King said.

"I'm sure some Westcarolina residents will buy liquor and wine over the border in Charlotte or by mail. We don't have the workforce or the desire to police that. But I believe that faithful church supporters and most residents will abide by the new plan and drink only beer from Westcarolina businesses if they choose to consume alcohol."

"Because we don't want to monopolize the beer industry, grocery stores and other businesses such as convenience stores can continue to sell all kinds of beer–as long as they reserve 50 percent of their offerings and shelf space to the fine beers made in Westcarolina."

King paused and looked into the camera with a self-satisfied expression. Many churchgoers in the Gastonia branch of God's Gift Church where he was preaching applauded loudly and some shouted, "Amen, brother."

Others looked upset and frustrated. Annie guessed they were angry that they couldn't obtain wine or liquor legally in Westcarolina. She'd talk to a few churchgoers coming out of the service.

King said breweries in different parts of the state would hold open houses for God's Gift church members to sample their products. He pointedly didn't include Westcarolina residents who weren't church members.

King wasn't finished.

"Those who can find nothing better to do than to criticize us, especially Annie Price of the *Charlotte Press*, will regret their negativity and Christ will lead them to a God's Gift church. Until then, we'll do our best to ignore a news industry that exists to put us down and kill the dreams of a God-centered state."

Annie was stunned that King had referred to her by name in a pejorative way. She'd not had that kind of public put-down since some of her more controversial stories in Texas. Though some reporters would enjoy public criticism, she preferred to do her job quietly and let the stories speak for themselves.

After a closing hymn that ended the broadcast, many church members rushed the stage to congratulate King and voice their support for the purchase of the lucrative breweries.

She stopped a departing churchgoer who identified himself as Ron Starr. He had looked increasingly disgruntled as King talked about the bans on liquor and wine sales.

"There are plenty of people in Westcarolina who enjoy liquor and wine. Why should they have to go to Charlotte to buy it? I think King is putting his philosophy ahead of what citizens might want. He also seems to forget that not all Westcarolinia residents are God's Gift members."

Starr paused for a moment and looked at Annie.

"I didn't like that King called you out and tried to intimidate you. Picking on a woman in the family way is not very sporting."

Despite the comments of Starr and a few others, the churchgoers' overwhelmingly positive reaction to King's announcement surprised Annie and Jim.

At Westcarolina's offices in Gastonia, Rob Ryland pumped his fist into the air and high-fived his aide, Ben Turner. He had feared a backlash against King's change in philosophy and the surprise purchase of the breweries. He guessed he shouldn't have worried. King could get away with a lot, given the adulation he enjoyed from his churchgoers.

Rob was glad that King had demonized the press, especially Annie, in public. Perhaps King was over what Rob thought was a ridiculous crush on the reporter.

Of course, he admitted to himself, he still wanted Annie, too.

CHAPTER 33

Annie was bone tired. The alcohol story had taken a lot out of her. She was nearly eight months pregnant, and the baby was kicking her unmercifully every night, making sleep difficult. She'd promised Jake she'd come to Austin to spend a couple of days with him and his children. If she waited much longer, she was afraid that the airlines would refuse to let her fly.

She made her plans to fly in on a Saturday and come back on a Monday night, which was the schedule Jake usually kept. He could have Saturday and Sunday with her and the children and most of Monday with his fellow partners at the Austin-based firm. She'd go to the office and do her own work. Annie had earned a lot of comp time with the hours she'd worked recently. The newspaper, like most in the industry, preferred to pay back extra hours worked with comp time rather than overtime to save money. It was a murky legal strategy, but most did it anyway.

She was really looking forward to the trip, to spend time with Jake's kids and get back to Austin, one of her favorite cities in Texas.

Jake met her at the Austin airport with Ashley, Hayley, and Jason. Five-year-old Jason, a little blond sprite, wrapped his chubby arms around her legs and said he'd show her his room at the condo.

"I have four goldfish," he said proudly. "You'll like them."

"I know I will," Annie told him.

Ashley, 10, and Hayley, 8, were much more subdued. Annie thought it might be difficult for them to see Jake hugging and kissing a woman they barely knew. They'd been at the wedding, of course, but probably were struggling with whether accepting her was disloyal to their mother. Jake's ex-wife had recently married one of his former law partners, and it was all a bit confusing to them, Annie thought. When couples divorced, it likely had a long-term, even lifelong, effect on the children. Her heart ached for them. Annie knew, of course, that she wasn't the cause of the split. It was Jake's wife's infidelity. Jake would never, ever say anything negative to them about their mother.

Throughout the afternoon, Annie worked hard to win the children's trust. They all walked on the wooded path behind the condo, stopping at the playground to let Jason climb up and slide down a dizzyingly high slide, Annie thought. Of course, he wanted to do it again and again, so she tried to get comfortable with a five-year-old's idea of fun.

In the afternoon, Annie played board games with the girls while Jason took a nap. She sat on the floor with the two dark-haired, brown-eyed girls, but when it came time to get off the floor, Jake had to practically lift her up to the sofa. The girls took it all in before shyly asking questions about the baby.

"It's a little girl, so it'll be another sister for you," Annie told them.

"What's her name?" Hayley asked.

"We haven't decided yet. What would you like us to name her?"

"Rapunzel," Hayley replied promptly. "She'll have long, beautiful hair like the girl in the story."

"That's silly," Ashley said to her younger sister. "Nobody is named Rapunzel. I like Victoria Eliza Susanna Satterfield. That sounds like a princess."

"Indeed, it does," Annie said. "We will keep those names in mind."

On the sofa, Jake smiled and tried to keep from laughing. Annie knew he was proud of his girls and the cute things they said.

The baby started kicking and Annie put their small hands on her belly. They were wide-eyed as they felt the reverberations.

"She wants to come out and meet you in person," Annie said, smiling.

"When?" they said in unison.

"Soon, maybe a month. Before Halloween," Annie said.

The girls both seemed excited, showing genuine warmth toward Annie after touching her pregnant belly.

Soon it was time to go to dinner, and Jake had promised them all Tex-Mex food at a downtown restaurant. Congress, Austin's primary street, sloped upward toward the majestic old Capitol building centered at the top of the hill. It was hard for Annie to navigate. But they arrived at the restaurant before she got winded.

They requested patio seating, since it wasn't overly hot that day. Soon, the blare of a mariachi band filled the air, and the musicians headed straight to them. The kids all looked at each other excitedly.

"This is for the little mama," one of the mariachi players said to Annie. They launched into a catchy Mexican lullaby that made restaurant patrons pause and listen. There was a groundswell of applause as Jake handed the leader some folded bills. The mariachis moved back inside the restaurant, playing as they left.

"That was great," Annie said to Jake. "Of course, it feels weird to be the center of attention. I'm not used to it."

"You're too retiring," Jake said. "A beautiful woman like you should feel good about being noticed."

"I guess it's because I'm a reporter. I'm used to sitting in a corner and observing quietly."

"You're going to be a mother and that brings attention on its own. You'd better get used to it."

Annie ordered a virgin margarita and chicken enchiladas with mole sauce, a traditional dish made with a bitter chocolate sauce. It was something she couldn't get easily in Charlotte, where Mexican food tended toward rather ordinary tacos and burritos. Jake had a Tex-Mex style steak and the kids all had children's taco plates. Everyone ate heartily, especially the girls.

That night, Jake said he was happy with how his children reacted to her and felt that they'd create a good, blended family. He made gentle love to her and stroked her belly softly. She wondered how she could be any happier.

The next day, they all dressed up and went to a German Catholic church near Austin. The men's choir, in the loft above the congregation, stood and belted out hymns with booming enthusiasm, much more so than some of the pallid denominations Annie had tried in the past.

"We're in the Hill Country," Jake said, as she remarked on the German flavor of the service. "Remember who settled it, mostly German-born immigrants. I'll take you back to Fredericksburg when we have time. You probably remember, some of the older people still speak German, although it's flavored with Texanisms."

"Yeah, I love that place. I love so much about Texas. Remind me again why I live in North Carolina."

"North Carolina is beautiful," Jake said. "After the baby comes, the three of us will visit more of the scenic parts of Westcarolina. Maybe we can squeeze in a day or two of travel before she comes."

"Meanwhile, we can enjoy the moment here," he added.

The rest of the day was a reprise of the day before, with plenty of outdoor and indoor play with the kids. Late in the afternoon, it was time to take them back to Jake's ex-wife.

They piled into Jake's SUV, which he kept in Austin in the garage of his condo. They drove about five miles to a suburb with large lots where Jake had once lived with his wife. The house was a low-slung, modernist ranch with floor to ceiling windows in the front and back. It had spectacular views of the grassy hills beyond.

"I had an architect design that house," Jake said. "I loved every inch of it. Now I look at it and I don't have any feelings at all. Your little cottage feels more like home."

By that time, the kids were out of the SUV and a slender, petite woman in white slacks and a navy sweater was hugging them. She'd met Jeannie, Jake's ex-wife, briefly before, but Jake re-introduced them. The woman barely acknowledged Annie.

The kids all hugged Annie before she and Jake left, and she promised she'd be back soon.

She felt both relieved and sad. Relieved that she'd passed muster with Jake's children and that she and Jake now could have some couples' time. Sad that she probably wouldn't see the kids again until after the baby was born. She thought being a stepmother was complicated.

That night, as she snuggled against Jake, she looked forward to one more day in Austin.

CHAPTER 34

The last day, Annie went with Jake to his law office, taking her laptop to work while he held meetings with the other partners. He had promised to take her to lunch at a romantic French restaurant and she was looking forward to it, even though she couldn't drink Sancerre, her favorite French white wine.

Around 11, she was winding down a productive morning in a borrowed office when Jake stopped by, saying there were several lawyer friends in the lobby he wanted her to meet. They walked out and met a couple who worked together as lawyers. It was a hurried introduction, but Annie sensed she would like them if she knew them better.

Then Maggie Mahaffey walked in.

Maggie had once worked on Annie's team at the *Houston Times*. Annie had thought she had promise but was always on the lookout for a better job. An Austin television station had hired her to be a reporter and part-time anchor. Annie frankly had been glad not to have to supervise her anymore or have any dealings with her at the *Times*. Maggie was just out for Maggie, she'd always thought.

The younger woman was a petite blonde whose signature color was pink. Today she wore hot pink cowboy boots, a short pink skirt and a filmy white blouse that showed more than a little cleavage. Her makeup was pink-toned and perfect. Annie felt dowdy in comparison in a navy maternity dress with military touches. When she'd looked in the mirror that morning, she'd been pleased. Not anymore. She felt like a very large lump.

"Why, Annie," Maggie said with a manufactured smile. "I didn't know you were coming to Austin. I'm sure Jake's kids were happy to see you finally. My goodness, you're huge. Not expecting twins, are you?"

Even for Maggie, this was beyond the pale, Annie thought. She resolved not to rise to the bait.

"Hi, Maggie. Yes, the children were wonderful. I'm almost to my eighth month, but no, we're not having twins. What are you doing here—in need of a little legal advice?"

"No, things are going great at the station," Maggie said. "I thought Jake would take me out to lunch."

"What made you think that?" Annie said, as Jake pretended to look at some legal papers.

"He often does on the Mondays he's in town, don't you, Jakie?"

"I wouldn't say often," Jake said, looking stricken. "I would say sometimes."

"Well, today he's taking me out to lunch," Annie said in a firm voice. "It was nice to see you, Maggie."

"Is he taking you to that French place?" Maggie said. "It's so romantic."

Hmmm, thought Annie. Why was he taking Maggie to the same romantic French restaurant he'd reserved for her? She nodded her head, refusing to let Maggie see her annoyance.

Jake stepped up and took Annie's arm, leading her out the door before the two women could have more conversation.

"Bye, Maggie," he said. "Call me later about the press conference. I'll check in with the other partners." Maggie sometimes offered the law firm important press releases she'd gotten on legal matters. The law firm had tapped Jake as its media liaison.

As they walked to the car, Annie and Jake were both quiet. Finally, she looked at him with reproach.

"I didn't know that you still saw Maggie," she said. "She made it sound like you're in constant touch."

"Baby, you know how she is. She likes to make things sound worse than they are."

"Are you sleeping with her?"

"No, I haven't slept with her since you told me you were pregnant and we decided to get married," Jake said. "You shouldn't get upset over Maggie. I've never felt about her the way I feel about you, and I've broken it off several times. She's just disappointed that I didn't marry her, but I never seriously considered it."

"Why do you take her out to lunch at romantic places?"

"She just shows up at lunchtime now and then, and I get roped into it," Jake said. "She tells me where she'd like to go." His face mirrored the misery that Annie was feeling.

"Do you kiss her?" Annie said, determined to know the painful truth.

"I've kissed her hello on the cheek. Believe me, it's not a big deal. It's you I love, not Maggie," he added.

"You were seeing Mr. West Texas before you moved and we got married," he pointed out. "Neither one of us was exclusive."

"I gave up Tom Marr when I found out I was pregnant by you. I didn't even see him before I left Houston," she said. "It seems like Maggie's leading you around and it's just a matter of time until you succumb to her wiles again."

"I think you're being very unfair to me, Annie," he said. "You know I've been enthusiastic about the baby, though I didn't plan on becoming a father again at my age."

Tears welled up in Annie's eyes and she sat down on a sofa in the lobby, looking gutted. She wished she'd never come to Austin. Jake's words about becoming a father again hurt her.

"Jake, take me back to the condo so I can pack. It's obvious we should spend some time apart. I just don't want to see you for a while."

"What about the baby?" Jake looked panicked.

"She'll be born, with or without you. I just need some time alone to think about all of this."

Later in the afternoon, Jake took Annie to the airport to make sure she got on the plane safely.

"Don't do this to us, Annie," he said with a pleading look. "You know I love you and our baby."

"You need to decide if you want to be married to me. That would preclude hanging out with Maggie and her ilk. I expect fidelity and I'm also tired of the endless flirting." She sidestepped his hug and moved toward the security line.

"Call me in a week and let's see where things are," she said with a coldness she couldn't have imagined a few hours before. Inside, she felt like lying down on the tile floor and bawling.

She almost wished that the plane would crash and put her out of her misery.

CHAPTER 35

A week later, King Avery called Annie and invited her to lunch at his Blowing Rock mansion. He said he had some questions and wanted to present them to her in person.

Annie listlessly pulled on a maroon stretchy dress for her lunch with King. The dress was growing tighter by the day, but she didn't want to invest in more maternity clothes. She didn't really care what she wore. But she brightened up the rather drab dress by putting on a gold necklace and earrings.

Since she'd left Jake in Austin, her mood had veered between angry and sad. She couldn't believe he'd fooled around with Maggie for as long as he apparently did. Maggie was a temptress who would stop at nothing to get what she wanted. The proof was that she kept hanging around Jake in her low-cut blouses. And Jake had hurt Annie badly when he said he didn't plan on becoming a father again, implying that he wasn't particularly happy about it. Should she give up now or fight for her marriage? She didn't want her daughter to grow up without the steadying presence of a father.

Those dismal thoughts swamped her on the two-hour drive to King's office in Blowing Rock. She didn't even gaze at the scenery, the majestic blue mountains in the clouds and the forest beginning to show a little fall color. She got out of her car, moving slowly, and resolved to be upbeat during the luncheon interview.

King wasn't taking her to a fancy French restaurant like Jake had been doing with Maggie. It was just a quick office lunch to discuss a story, she reasoned. He wasn't a boyfriend, or a former boyfriend. He was a newsmaker, and sometimes an unpleasant one. She wished she hadn't made an issue of Jake's lunches with Maggie because she'd often had lunch with sources.

King greeted her with a firm handshake, the kind where he enveloped her hand with both of his to make it more personal. She supposed that he'd learned all the ways to make parishioners feel good during his years in the ministry.

"First," he said, "I want to apologize. I've prayed a lot about last week and I know I shouldn't have criticized you in front of our large congregation. I promise I won't ever do that again."

"Apology accepted," Annie said. "As a reporter, I've been called out too many times to count. I was just surprised you would do that. As a man of the cloth, I would expect you to have more tolerance."

"I usually do, Annie Price," he said. "Somehow, I was angrier about the alcohol issue than I should have been. My congregation has been very supportive overall.

"But enough of that," he said. "I invited you for a different, and hopefully more pleasant, discussion.

"Follow me to the little dining room," he added. "It's designed for small lunches, which work well sometimes. Do you like chicken salad and fresh fruit? I hope so, because that's what we're having. I thought it sounded healthy for a pregnant woman."

King was fussing over her like a mother hen, she thought irritably. She didn't like it when sources or co-workers referred to her pregnancy as a disease of sorts. It made her sound less than competent at her job. But she confirmed that she very much liked chicken salad.

"Where's Rob?" she asked. "It seems like you're always together."

"He went to one of our churches in Asheville to give a talk to a women's group. He's becoming quite good at melding the Scripture with everyday concerns."

Annie breathed a sigh of relief. She didn't want to see Rob and hear his gibes when she was feeling so vulnerable.

"I had several reasons for asking you to lunch," King said during their first course of tomato soup. "I'd like you to come to work for me as our director of communications. It's a role that's vacant right now and needs to be filled with someone smart and diplomatic. You'd work for the state but would also have some duties with the church.

"Whatever the Press is paying you, we'd double it."

Annie was surprised, and for a minute or two, intrigued. She'd just found out that her partner Jim had been reassigned to the general news desk. He could help her out when she badly needed him, but the new owners were stretching the already-thin news staff. So much for the promise that no one would be laid off. Instead, they seemed to reassign a bunch of reporters to work harder and longer. She would have to cover Westcarolina alone.

But she quickly dismissed the idea of working for Westcarolina and King, thinking of at least two things that deterred her. She'd have to join or at least embrace God's Gift Church. She didn't believe in many of its principles, such as its anti-abortion policies. Also, she'd be under Rob's thumb because he was lieutenant governor.

"King, I appreciate the generous offer, but I've always been a journalist, and I probably always will. It's my nature to seek the truth, and in your organization, I might not have the freedom to do that."

King looked crestfallen but didn't argue with her.

"Somehow, I thought that's what you'd say."

He ticked off the most recent God's Gift success. The judge assigned to what Annie thought of as the beer case had put everything on hold. But King's lawyers thought from the court papers filed that she'd probably rule in their favor. It didn't matter to the judge that God's Gift owned fifteen mega-breweries and was dedicating 90 percent to the state and keeping ten percent, King mused.

Westcarolina Wiccans had gone completely underground, as far as King knew. None had joined the church or moved out of the new state. Gone were the Wiccan celebrations like May Day, erasing a colorful tradition that most Asheville residents enjoyed.

"That was a misfire on your part," she told King.

"It was really Rob's idea," he said. "He's put a lot of thought into what a new state like Westcarolina can do."

"Well, I hope he's not elected as a four-year lieutenant governor," Annie said.

"What's with you and Rob?" King asked.

"Let's just say I've seen his true colors."

"Can you come back here one more time, perhaps next week?" King asked. "Something I'd like to show you and a person I'd like you to meet isn't quite ready yet. I know it's a lot to ask, but it's still a while before your due date, right?"

"I've got a month, so yes, I'll come back, maybe next week," she said. "I'm slowing down some at work, but new initiatives in Westcarolina are still a priority."

She got up to leave and King came around to walk her out. He seemed to want to prolong the visit as much as possible. She wasn't eager to get back on the road and go home to an empty house, either.

"How's Jake? Is he getting excited about the baby?"

The question brought tears to her eyes, and to her horror, she started crying full blast. King enveloped her in a sympathetic hug, which quickly turned into something else. He kissed her on the mouth, his full lips soft and lingering. She could smell the light musky cologne he was wearing and feel his broad shoulders. Annie enjoyed it for about a half minute before she broke away. She looked him in his amazing blue eyes and tried to decipher what she saw. He couldn't take his eyes off her, either.

"I'm sure you can tell that I have feelings for you, Annie."

"King, I hear you, but this must never happen again. I'm married and my job depends on covering you objectively. Jim, my partner, got reassigned, so it's just me. I don't want to be constantly afraid that you'll break the boundaries between you and me. I could get fired if we did. Things between us must stay professional."

"I could feel that you liked it, Annie," he said. "You're a great kisser, by the way."

"That's neither here nor there," she said. "I'll talk to you soon."

She walked to her car, looking back once to see him waving.

Thinking about the incident as she drove home, she felt guilty. She'd cried in front of a source, and he took advantage of the vulnerability she'd shown. She'd enjoyed his passionate kissing and hadn't stopped it soon enough. Did that make her conduct any better than Jake's? Yes, she decided. She'd never sleep with King or any of his staff.

As soon as she got home, she called Jake and said she missed him terribly. He sounded contrite and happy that she'd called.

"Please come back to Charlotte. I need you and want you here for the birth of our little girl. All I ask is that you stop seeing Maggie, and anyone else in your past," she said.

"Done. I'll be on a plane tomorrow, baby."

CHAPTER 36

"You look more beautiful each day and I've missed you like crazy," he said. "Why don't you stay home this afternoon and let me show it?"

"I love you, Jake, but I need to get back to work. We'll have all night together."

Jake suggested going to their favorite Italian restaurant when she got home, and she quickly agreed. She was determined that things be as normal and positive as they could be.

Over dinner, they talked about the baby, her lavender nursery and names. He laughed again about Hayley's suggestion of Rapunzel for their baby girl's name. His children obviously made him happy and proud. Annie knew she was lucky to have him as the father of her daughter. She couldn't shake off the memory of his words about not being ready to be a father again.

In fact, they were tiptoeing around each other, aware that there was a fissure in their marriage that had to be repaired. Annie had decided not to bring up the subject of Maggie again and to trust that he'd given up contact with her.

Annie's newfound tolerance was partly because of the kiss she'd shared with King. If she was being honest with herself, she'd freely admit that she'd enjoyed it a little too much. The more she got to know him, the more attractive she found him. She guessed that was the inevitable result when a handsome man like King declared feelings for her, especially with her swelling body. She didn't think she was unattractive, exactly, but she'd always taken pride in her slender figure. As her body kept getting larger, she didn't really recognize herself in the mirror. Her face was getting moon shaped. She was getting uncomfortable in ways she hadn't expected. Just recently, her ankles had begun to swell, leaving her with only one pair of shoes that fit.

She wondered if part of her appeal to King stemmed from the fact that she looked very pregnant, and he'd never see Claire with child. She wished she knew how much their childlessness had diminished their relationship. It would help to explain his over-the-top behavior toward her.

Annie busied herself the next few days with routine tasks, one of which was to sit down at work with Jim and talk about the issues she was leaving him to pick up for stories. While she was out on maternity leave, probably about two months, her fellow reporter would be moved from general assignment back to cover Westcarolina.

Jim had put a good face on it when his editor originally ordered him to return to general assignment because of staff cuts. He joked about being on the animal beat, writing stories about errant snakes, greedy coyotes, and sleazy puppy farms. Those types of stories weren't important, but they generated a lot of computer clicks.

He'd urged Annie to take more than two months off.

"I'm not saying that so I can spend more time on the Westcarolina beat," he said with seriousness. "This will be the biggest thing you've ever experienced, and you should take full advantage of it. I know my wife did."

"Thanks, Jim," she said. "A former boyfriend told me the same thing. He said at the end of the day, I'd value raising my child a lot more than collecting a bigger pile of newspaper clippings. I'm eager to see what it feels like to be a mother."

A few days later, she grabbed a reporter's notebook, kissed Jake goodbye and prepared to drive to King's Blowing Rock mansion one last time. He'd promised her an important story.

"Are you sure you should go?" Jake asked. "It's less than a month before your due date."

"I feel great," Annie said. "Besides, I need one more outing before I'm cooped up at home for a couple of months."

"You shouldn't think of it like that," Jake said. "I think you'll enjoy being home with our baby and I'll take care of you both."

Annie valued his concern, but she also felt he was being slightly paternalistic. Sometimes she felt that people who'd had children acted like they had a big secret she couldn't possibly understand. She loved the thought of becoming a mother, but she hoped she wouldn't get smug about it.

"I get restless sometimes when I can't get out and do things. You know how I am," she said.

"Don't worry about that. I'll make sure you can get out of the house when you're climbing the walls."

She gladly left the city behind. She'd always enjoyed the solitude of traveling somewhere, occupied with her own thoughts, and watching the scenery. Since it was a Wednesday midmorning, there was little traffic, and the trip was quick. When she got to the Blowing Rock mansion, King greeted her with a smile, a quick handshake and beckoned her into his large living room.

"Since it's almost time for lunch, I suggest we talk in the private dining room while we eat the delicious Quiche Lorraine and fruit Rosa has prepared," King said. "I was thinking you'd need some protein and vitamins."

Oh no, he was being a mother hen again, almost like Jake. She forced herself not to say anything, but she wished he'd stop it.

Annie stood up to follow him into the dining room and a torrent of water burst out of her.

She turned red until she figured out what was happening.

"King, my water has broken. I'll need to go to the hospital. Can you take me?"

"Sure. Of course." He sounded perfectly accommodating and happy to be needed, but nervous. Annie didn't blame him–she was also unnerved and almost undone at the thought that the baby was coming so soon. She'd been foolish to undertake a road trip, albeit just a day trip. She'd wanted one last big story to prove herself before disappearing for a few months.

"Do you have a blanket you can spread on the front seat, so it won't get wet?" she asked.

"No problem," he said, sounding more in charge. "I should have thought of that myself."

He left briefly and brought back two soft blue blankets. She hurried out with him. King spread one blanket on the passenger side of his black BMW and held her hand to help her into the seat. He made sure she put her seat belt on, albeit fastened under her large midsection. He wrapped the other blanket around her.

"We have the wonderful Watauga Regional Medical Center nearby where I've visited new mothers and babies often," he said. "You'll get great care."

When they arrived at the emergency department, a nurse put Annie in a wheelchair while King walked at her side. They got to the labor and delivery floor where several nurses knew King from previous visits.

"Who have you got for us today, Rev. King? Is she a God's Gift church member?" the head nurse said.

"As a matter of fact, she's a friend from Charlotte who has gone into labor while visiting in my home," King said. "I know you'll treat her right."

A nurse examined her briefly in a small room and said she wasn't far from delivery.

"We'll need to get a labor room set up and a nurse on call to come in to assist you. Lots of babies are coming today. Meanwhile, you can stay in the maternity waiting room."

Annie called Jake right away, while King stepped away to give them privacy.

"Oh, Jake," she said with nervousness in her voice. "I'm at the Watauga Regional Medical Center in Blowing Rock. My water broke, and the nurse says I'll have Rapunzel in a few hours. Can you leave now?"

"You know it'll take me a couple of hours, but I'll get going right now," he said. "Is there anyone who can stay with you until I get there?"

"King Avery brought me here, and I think he'll stay a while."

"Okay. Ask him to say a few prayers for us. Just don't dance with him."

Annie giggled, remembering King's too-close dancing at his big party. She felt good that Jake could joke about it, instead of becoming unreasonably jealous.

"I love you, by the way," she said.

"You too, baby. I'm excited for us."

King came back and walked with her to the waiting room. They sat and waited for the next step.

"Can I stay with Ms. Price for a few minutes?" King asked when a nurse came in that he knew. "I've done this before with wives whose husbands are deployed in the military or out of town on business."

"Yes, but you'll have to leave soon," the nurse said. "She'll need her privacy for labor and delivery."

A searing pain wracked Annie as they waited. She groaned, and he squeezed her hand. She tried to make light of her discomfort. "If this is a contraction, I want no part of it."

To distract her, they talked about anything except the *Charlotte Press* and God's Gift Church. They laughed at each other's childhood tales and King's rueful stories about mistakes he'd made in his ministry. Annie enjoyed his entertaining–and alternately soothing–presence until the next contraction came along. She winced in pain, and he grabbed her hand again.

The nurse finally appeared.

"Okay, Reverend. Time for you to leave. If I'm not mistaken, she's going to give birth before long. You can stay in the waiting room if you'd like."

"You don't have to wait," Annie said. "Jake will be here in a couple of hours." Despite her weak protests, she hoped he'd stay.

"I will not leave you alone, Annie. I'll be in the waiting room."

"Thanks, King," Annie said, glad that she'd have someone there if things went awry.

A nurse directed her to a labor room, where an experienced nurse held her hand and soothed her during increasingly close contractions. Less than an hour later, she was taken to a delivery room where she gave birth to a healthy girl. It was painful, but short-lived. The infant weighed 6 pounds, 3 ounces, had dark hair and an expression that already looked alert.

Annie was thrilled with the baby's first cry. It was as close to a peak experience as she'd ever had. Jim and Tom had been right. She felt that no story she'd ever written had left her as happy and full of pride as birthing her child.

A new nurse took her and her daughter to a room where she nursed the baby for the first time. The infant got the hang of it quickly, latching on to her breast hungrily.

"Your husband is waiting at the door. Shall I call him in to see the baby?" the nurse asked.

She nodded, not willing to take her eyes off her beautiful infant.

Instead of Jake, the "husband" turned out to be King, bearing an enormous bouquet of fall flowers and a huge smile.

Annie was embarrassed and quickly pulled up the sheet to cover her naked breasts and nursing infant.

"Don't worry. I've seen so many women nursing that I'm immune to the sight. It's part of God's plan."

The baby stopped nursing and Annie could see that she was drifting off to sleep.

"Can I hold her for just a moment?" King asked. Annie handed her over, and he cradled the little girl in his enormous hands.

"You seem like a natural father," Annie said. "Why didn't you and Claire have children?"

"She didn't want any," King said with what Annie thought was sadness. "It takes two, you know."

There was a knock at the door, and Jake walked in. He looked surprised—and not altogether happy--to see King holding their daughter.

"Here's your little bundle of joy," King said as he transferred the baby to Jake. "She's so beautiful."

Jake's face softened as he gazed at the sleeping baby. "Yes, she is. I appreciate your staying with Annie while I was trying to get here."

King got the none-too-subtle hint and said his goodbyes.

"Annie, call me the day you get back to work," he said. "I'll have some good stories waiting."

She was glad that King had steered the conversation past the personal to their work relationship. Jake probably felt envious that King had been there instead of him.

"Thanks for everything, King. I appreciate all you did for me."

CHAPTER 37

Annie and Jake named their daughter Anna Price Satterfield, as suggested by Jake. He liked using both of their last names and the similarity of Anna to Annie. Annie was enjoying her maternity leave—the ability to spend more time with Jake and, most of all, cuddling and feeding Anna. She thought the infant's dark hair and long body were like hers. The shape of their daughter's nose and mouth were all Jake. She hadn't known that becoming a mother would fill her with so much delight. Even with all the midnight feedings and other work Anna required, Annie wished she could have another child. She guessed that her desire was mostly hormones at work. At her age, she knew it was just a lucky fluke that she'd become pregnant. She resolved to enjoy Anna to the fullest, even if she had to cut back on her job.

It turned out that Tom Marr, her former West Texas lover, was prescient when he told her she should have a baby or two. Giving birth to Anna was sort of like birthing a major investigative series. The satisfaction of producing life-changing stories was short-lived compared to knowing that she'd have this adored child for life.

It wasn't all thrilling; she realized as she changed dirty diapers and worried about Anna's bouts with colic. There was nothing worse than a baby's nonstop crying, she thought.

Annie became inured to Jake's twice-monthly visits to Austin, trying to put Maggie Mahaffey and the young woman's pink wardrobe in the back of her mind. She hadn't forgotten it, however. In her heart, Jake was on probation, and she wasn't sure what to do about it. Time, she guessed, would ease her bruised feelings. She missed him greatly when he was gone, because, true to his word, he took care of her and Anna. He fixed wonderful meals, handled visitors when she was too tired to see them, and brought Anna to her for middle-of-the-night feedings.

She wondered how Jake was feeling about the marriage and new parenthood, but she wasn't willing to go beneath the surface with him just yet. He acted pleased, but was he really happy? When they were dating, she could slough off any angry or hurt feelings toward Jake by seeing Tom, who was as steady and open as they came. But though he'd sent a beautiful set of antique baby silverware in response to the birth announcement, he'd gone silent—and she didn't feel it was fair to contact him beyond her thank-you note.

One thing she could do and did—was to refuse to buy Anna any pink clothes. Though she tried not to think about Maggie, she didn't need reminders of her stupid pink wardrobe. Little dark-headed Anna looked better in red and other bright colors, she reasoned.

With the two-month maternity leave nearly up, Annie had mixed feelings. She'd enjoyed it much more than she thought she would. But some of her old restlessness was stirring. She knew she could go back to work comfortably after hiring Sylvia, an older woman with impeccable credentials who'd take care of Anna. With Annie's flexible schedule, she could come home often for lunch and breast-feed the baby or express milk for her.

Jake had rented an office in uptown Charlotte because Anna had taken over his study, but he came home much of the day to help with childcare. If Annie had been alone with the baby all the time, her leave would have been much less satisfying.

With Jake sometimes working at home, he and Annie could both see how inadequate her small cottage was for them, plus a baby.

They spent several lunch hours with a realtor looking at houses and found one they both liked. It was in the Myers Park area of Charlotte, close to uptown, which had older, majestic homes. They bought a 1920s Italianate villa with four bedrooms, four baths and a large, remodeled kitchen. They both loved the outdoor area with its pool, barbecue equipment and huge patio. The price made Annie gasp. She knew Jake did very well financially, but his salary and bonus seemed up in the stratosphere. Annie hadn't known because she and Jake rarely discussed money. To some extent, they kept separate finances, except that he paid most of the bills and she used hers for clothes and other expenses for work.

To tell the truth, Annie realized Jake liked the expensive house better than she did. He liked showy houses, while she knew she was going to miss her little Craftsman cottage in an artsy area of Charlotte. Their move would take place soon, and since Annie was headed back to work the next week, Jake would take charge of supervising it.

She picked up their mail and noticed an envelope from King Avery. She opened it and found a handwritten note from him. He again expressed his congratulations for the birth–he'd sent her a card soon after she took Anna home from the Blowing Rock hospital. He also asked when she'd return to work and indicated he'd like her to talk to him "about a matter of great importance as soon as you get back."

She called his direct number, and he answered immediately.

"Annie," he said with warmth in his voice, "Jim Markham told me you'd be returning to work next week. Is that right?"

"Yes," she said, happy to hear a friendly, adult voice after a day of Anna crying and refusing to sleep.

"When can you come to Blowing Rock? I'd like to offer you a big story and want you to meet a top employee involved in it."

Annie thought for a moment. She needed a few days to catch up with paperwork, her bosses and fellow reporters.

"I get back on Monday. How about Wednesday?"

"Fine," he said with enthusiasm in his voice. "If you can, be here at 11:30 and we'll have lunch first."

"Are you sure?" she asked. "The last time we were about to have lunch, you had to take me to the hospital."

He laughed with surprise at her teasing. "I don't think there's another baby about to be born, is there? How's the little girl? What did you name her?"

"Her name is Anna Price Satterfield. You may hear her crying in the background."

"A beautiful name for a beautiful girl," he said with a wistfulness she felt was genuine.

"Thank you. I'll see you Wednesday."

She hung up and smiled to herself. She must admit that she enjoyed joking with King. Many initially formal relationships with a journalist's sources turned more relaxed over time, but maybe hers with King was over the top. She wondered if he was filling a void left by her lingering resentment toward Jake. She resolved not to let positive feelings toward King affect her hard-hitting coverage.

Jim, her friend and fellow reporter who was covering Westcarolina during her leave, had told her that King's presence at the hospital's maternity ward had caused quite a stir. A gossipy nurse spread the word that she saw King holding hands with a heavily pregnant reporter for the *Press*–the same one he had criticized in public.

King made it known that Annie had been waiting for her husband and he had simply stayed with her until Jake arrived.

However, the damage to King–and to her sources who'd heard about it–had lingered, Jim said.

CHAPTER 38

On a December Monday, Annie got ready for the hectic week ahead. Pursuing her much-loved work and being around adults all day had its charms. On one hand, she hated to leave Anna. On the other, once she knew Anna would be fine with her babysitter, she missed the company of coworkers who'd become friends. Sara, Jim, Amanda and a few others had come by to see her and Anna, bringing gifts (a few of them pink, to Annie's chagrin) and office news. But the loneliness that had followed those friendly visits would often last all day.

As she struggled to find something in her closet that flattered her still-large, post-pregnancy figure, she thought about how universal her feelings were about going back to the office. Women around the world felt torn when they had to leave their babies, but she was luckier than most. She had a job that mattered to her, and good childcare. She'd read a lot recently about how women in some Asian countries declined to have children because of the dearth of jobs that satisfactorily covered the costs of childcare. In another part of the world, studies had shown that Scandinavian women were happier than most other mothers because the government provided childcare and other benefits for free.

She wished that the U.S. government would provide free, good childcare to all women, but she had to be glad that she and Jake made enough money to afford the high cost of hiring someone. Women who toiled in blue-collar jobs weren't as lucky.

She needed to focus on her closet search. After holding up clothes in front of her figure, she settled on her best stretchy black pants with a long red blouse. She added some silver jewelry and came through the living room, where Jake greeted her with his trademark wolf whistle.

"How fat do I look?" Annie asked in the time-honored words of new mothers.

"Are you kidding? Mama Mia, you look sexy as hell," he said.

Annie smiled with appreciation.

"I guess that's why I keep you around. You've always made me feel beautiful." She wondered for a moment if that was true. It was one thing she appreciated about him. Many men she'd dated seemed oblivious to what she wore and never commented on her appearance.

"Baby, the way you look today, you're the most beautiful woman I've ever seen."

Annie drove to work in a good mood she hoped would last all day.

Hugs, warm words, and a special group lunch at a Southern-themed restaurant greeted her return. As she enjoyed crisp fried squash and scrumptious cornbread, she thought about how happy she was to have caring colleagues. The difference between Charlotte and Houston was that most of the Charlotteans were older with families and could rarely get together outside of work. But it was nice to go out occasionally for group lunches. That was okay, she mused. She was in a stage of life that was sweet—and overdue.

Jim, who'd shepherded the Westcarolina beat during her leave, had surprisingly little to report. He gave her a file of mostly routine follow-ups to previous stories, such as the beer controversy. There was very little reporting of fresh stories.

"I'm sure King was waiting for you to get back," Jim said. "If I didn't know you and Jake, I'd think there was something going on between you and King. I don't think there's any doubt that he has a crush on you."

"Unfortunately, I think you're right," Annie said with a sigh. "It makes my job a little more difficult. I don't think it would be a problem if he had a woman who acted more like a minister's wife."

"Yeah, I've heard the same things you have," Jim said. "Wonder why they don't divorce?"

"I think it could become an issue with his more conservative church members. Also, I get the impression she wouldn't want to give up the status that comes with his mega-ministry."

"I suspect that he's a pretty lonely guy," Jim said. "Careful, Annie. Don't let him put you in a difficult position."

"Believe me, I'm aware of that," she said. "This is a job I love, and I'm treading lightly with the most important source on the beat."

She wondered exactly what Jim meant. He'd been the one who'd told her gossip was circulating about King's presence in the maternity ward the night Anna was born. Her fellow reporter would probably disapprove of King holding her hand during her contractions. But it was so innocent, she thought—the comfort a human would provide to another human in pain. She would carefully monitor her own behavior around King—for both of their sakes.

After a couple of days of catching up, she set out Wednesday for her appointment with King at his mountain office.

Her winter drive to Blowing Rock differed from that of the colorful fall, but just as beautiful in its own way. The sloping land giving way to the mountains, and the bare trees, a framework for vivid blue wintry skies, were majestic. Annie, who loved winter, appreciated the dusting of snow on the mountains. But something about that conversation with Jim had put a damper on the week.

She arrived at King's home, and he came out to greet her. He gave her his usual handshake, one hand under hers and the other hand on top. Annie thought he held her hand a little too long, but decided it wasn't worth worrying about.

He led her to the private dining room, where a server brought them a delicious Caesar salad and French onion soup. They made small talk for a few moments, then King moved into more meaty territory.

"I want to tell you about our next initiative. You know we're banning the sale of tobacco products all over Westcarolina. We've decided we'll replace those dreadful products with our home-grown marijuana."

Annie felt shocked but intrigued, contemplating the possibilities for a story. She kept a poker face, as she usually did in interviews where she saw a controversial subject. She'd found that her nonchalance encouraged people to tell her more.

"That's interesting," she said with a casual air. "How does your God's Gift congregation feel about growing and consuming marijuana?"

"Mostly, the church elders who know about our efforts are very supportive," King said. "We've been growing cannabis for a few years to sell in states where it's legal, including Colorado, Massachusetts and California.

"I want to introduce you to Farmer Ted, as we all call him."

They walked into the living room, where a tall, heavyset man dressed in worn jeans and a faded camouflage coat awaited them. He smiled as King introduced him to Annie.

"I believe it was about two months ago when I was supposed to meet you, and you had a baby instead," he said.

Annie felt his warmth and smiled.

"Yes, the timing of having my little girl in Blowing Rock wasn't ideal. But King was very helpful to me and my husband. My apologies for standing you up."

She quickly steered the conversation to his farming activities.

"How long have you worked for the church?" she asked.

"I've supervised the cannabis enterprise for about three years," he said. "We're lucky to have established markets that value our product, and we work hard at growing something special. The flavors we produce are fantastic, users in other states say."

He guided her to a table where three bowls of harvested cannabis were lined up. He pointed to each. "This is Smoky Mountains High, that one is Kill Devil Hills Delight, and we call the one on the end Ashe County Line. They are our three big sellers."

"Where do you cultivate it?"

"That's a well-kept secret," Farmer Ted said. "We have many growers and locations that we use throughout Westcarolina. If I told you about them, we'd have a lot of theft. Now that we have a state of our own, we can ramp up our production considerably. Would you like to try our products? We can make up a to-go box."

"No, thank you."

Annie, like most others of her generation, had tried pot, but all it did was to make her hungry and sleepy. She knew Jake would enjoy it, but her newspaper, like most others, prohibited reporters from taking expensive gifts, which it defined as anything worth more than $25. Depending on how they packaged it, she'd be taking a to-go box worth hundreds of dollars.

"How much marijuana do you produce?" she asked, coming out of her private thoughts.

"That varies year to year, but it's enough to provide several million dollars a year to God's Gift Church," he said. "We call our producers Growers for God. Sometimes they don't even want a share of the profits–they just consider the cannabis cultivation part of their ministry."

She was taking notes eagerly and didn't see King signaling to Farmer John that he'd take all the questions from there.

"Cannabis has indeed made a lot of money for our church, but most of it has gone into God's Gift charitable activities," King said. "Now, we will transfer the entire enterprise to the government of Westcarolina," King said. "It'll be used to fund activities, like social services, that will directly help citizens."

"Will it make up for the tax revenue the state would get from selling cigarettes?" Annie asked.

"It will definitely exceed it," King said. "We'll have licensed stores that carry only cannabis, as in other states and countries. Probably we'll use many of the ABC stores, since we won't be using them to sell liquor."

"The population in Westcarolina is predominantly conservative. Do you think they'll embrace the legalization and sale of marijuana?"

"Definitely. Once we clarify the financial advantages, there's no doubt about it. That doesn't mean that a majority of God's Gift members will use it. But that's all right. The market for selling it in other states is extremely profitable.

"Can I call you later with more questions? I need to get back to the office and launch the story with Jim," she told King.

"Of course. I'll be here at your disposal."

Annie said goodbye quickly and walked outside. She got into her car and used her cell phone for quick calls to her editor and Jim.

"You won't believe what they've done this time."

CHAPTER 39

Rob Ryland sat in the spacious office suite he used at King's Blowing Rock mansion. Since Rob had become lieutenant governor, he'd commandeered a much larger office area than his former cubbyhole next to King's. His office suite, one of several of the two executives used in Westcarolina, was across the cavernous living room. Sometimes he wished he was still at his previous office so that he could keep a better eye on King and his visitors—chiefly Annie Price.

Today, for instance, he read the banner headline of the Charlotte Press that screamed, Westcarolina trades cigarettes for cannabis. The multi-page package consisted of stories written by Annie and Jim. They'd interviewed most everyone connected with the issue—tobacco industry executives, cigarette retail sellers, God's Gift church members, non-church citizens, government executives in North Carolina, states that bought Westcarolina's marijuana, and so on.

Rob was angry—and increasingly frustrated. He believed King kept falling under the spell of Annie, who annoyingly seemed to know exactly how to play the pastor-governor. It was clear to Rob that Annie even liked King, while treating Rob as coldly as ever. In his more honest moments, he admitted to himself that he was horribly jealous that Annie directed all her attention to King and avoided any contact with the lieutenant governor's office. Would he ever rid himself of that woman, with her sexy body and incisive mind, consuming his thoughts?

In this frame of mind, he strode across the living room to King's office suite. He brushed past the administrative assistants and into the office where King was also reading the morning papers.

"Wow, Annie really outdid herself on this one," King said. "I didn't think it would be such a big deal."

"You didn't think, period," Rob replied. "Had she gotten a tip about this?"

"No, I told her because I knew it would come out when we officially ban cigarettes. The rollout starts next month. Better to be ahead of the story instead of surprised when it surfaces."

"Now that's one of the dumbest things I've ever heard."

King visibly bristled, frowned and answered Rob in a frosty voice.

"Rob, I don't like your tone or attitude. Remember who got you this job. If you don't like the way I do things, you're free to go back to West Texas and let somebody else become lieutenant governor."

Rob immediately knew he'd gone too far and adopted a more conciliatory tone.

"I didn't mean to be critical. I'm just upset that we'll waste the next few days talking to a bunch of reporters."

"I'll take the heat," King said. "You can go back to work on the other pieces, like figuring out all the tax angles. Also, we need to take applications from retail businesses in each county that want to sell the cannabis. We're going to use the former N.C. liquor locations to sell our beautiful product. We want to make them classy stores."

"Those store operators will have to pay the state dearly for that privilege," Rob said, sounding too happy about the prospect, in King's opinion.

"Just remember, we can't lose all the excellent money we make selling some of our crop yields to other states. We'll have to figure out some sort of balance."

Rob wouldn't admit it, but the whirlwind of public interest they'd unleashed took him aback. He suspected that King felt the same way.

Was it crazy to undertake such a large and potentially complicated initiative in their still-new state? Rob had spent a lot of time talking to officials in some places where cannabis was legal. The coldness he'd detected in some officials showed they were unhappy with the prospect of more competition. Rob, who often smoked pot, knew that

Westcarolina's products were superior to those in other states. For instance, Smoky Mountains High had an unusual, sweet taste that he thought came from being grown in the mountains. King, who didn't use it, had received assurances that their state would dominate the competition.

"I'd better return some media calls that are stacking up–from Asheville to Auckland." King said.

"Have you heard much from church members?"

"I haven't had time to take their temperature. That's one thing you can do, Rob. Call as many of the major church leaders as you can. You know who they are. Some of them have known about it and are fine with it," King said. "Maybe we should watch a little of the Raleigh TV coverage to see what's going on there."

He turned on the big-screen TV in King's office and they saw two of their biggest opponents being interviewed–Sam Waller, the N.C. state senator, and Ike Hinton, the powerful House member.

They were talking to Jane Spencer, a political reporter from a top Raleigh station.

"Sam, you may remember that we met during the hearings the North Carolina legislature held on Westcarolina's application to split off and become a separate state," Spencer said. "I remember that you and Ike Hinton opposed the proposal."

"Yes, and we were right considering all the bizarre things they've come up with as a new state," Waller said. "The latest thing, outlawing tobacco sales in favor of marijuana, is outrageous. The Westcarolina area is conservative. It's not California."

"No one knows the long-term effect of marijuana to those who use it," Hinton said. "I'm not sure I would want to drive there, or anywhere nearby, with all of those stoned people on the road."

Waller's voice got louder as he got angrier.

"Obviously God's Gift church broke North Carolina law by growing and selling it illegally, before Westcarolina became a state."

"The governor and lieutenant governor say they run a theocracy–anything that benefits the church is good government–and vice versa,

Hinton said. "Their state laws, now being written, will explicitly say that cultivating marijuana, using it and selling it are all perfectly legal."

Waller said the N.C. legislature still had a few options.

"Because the government officials of the new state keep coming up with crazy programs, we're going to ask the N.C. legislature to rescind approval for Westcarolina, and recommend that Congress do the same," Hinton said.

"We made a huge mistake," Waller added.

Whatever Rob expected from the two state legislators, this was worse, he thought. He wondered if there was any way to placate them enough to change their minds. Stop panicking, he told himself.

"Gentlemen, are you being too hasty?" the TV reporter asked. "You don't know how the cannabis initiative is going to play out. Why don't you wait and see before you do anything drastic?"

"We'll give them a month before we take any action," Waller said after some reflection. "We'll have to talk to a lot of legislators, anyway. But we'd better not hear of any other kooky initiatives."

King looked at Rob after the interview with Waller and Hinton had ended. He could see that the lieutenant governor was as shocked as he was.

"Those two were always against us," King said. "But I don't think they represent the bulk of the legislature."

Rob was thoughtful for a moment before his next words.

"Since they always seem to travel together, it's conceivable that Hinton and Waller could have a minor accident. Perhaps they'll run off a slick road, since it will probably snow again soon."

King looked alarmed.

"Rob, don't even think about it. Let's wait and see what happens. If something unfortunate should surface now, the blame would fall directly on us."

"Okay, but they shouldn't be allowed to destroy everything we've worked for."

CHAPTER 40

King drove through Gastonia to his office in the downtown area. Preferring to work in Blowing Rock at his larger, more luxurious home office, he came to the Westcarolina state capital as little as he could.

His Gastonia office was utilitarian, just a desk with some guest chairs, a conference room, some grip-and-grin pictures of groundbreakings and King with various celebrities.

King felt obliged to be seen by Westcarolina's government workers two or three times a week at the main building. To appear more serious, he even dressed in a sober-looking suit and tie, rather than his usual winter attire of jeans and a sweater. He was spending about 85 percent of his time on state business, having found decent leaders to take his place in God's Gift top administrative posts. He was less and less interested in taking the time for his church responsibilities, although he did a Sunday sermon that was beamed at all the church sites. Since a gifted minister in his flock wrote the sermons, they didn't require any heavy lifting. He thought that if he had to write his own sermons, he'd try to get out of the Sunday obligation. But delivering hope and hell in equal measures was what his congregations expected of him.

Today, he wasn't thinking about his church or Westcarolina. He was wondering how he could get Annie Price to visit him when his secretary buzzed him.

"There's a woman on line one who's very insistent about talking only to you. She says her name is Celia, but she won't give a last name. She says she must talk to you right now."

"Give me a minute," King said. "I'm trying to think of who she might be."

He racked his brain and could only come up with one person—Ceil Montgomery, the female part of the husband-and-wife team who'd bombed the abortion pill factory almost a year ago. Soon after the bombing, a tip to the FBI had described a middle-aged couple fleeing the scene in an old car that had turned out to be stolen. After the FBI publicized the tip, Ceil and Rad went into hiding in the far reaches of Westcarolina. They'd ditched the car after the crime.

He thought the call could only spell trouble. He picked up the phone.

"Hey, Ceil," he said, mustering some good cheer in his voice. "How are you and Rad?"

"Miserable," she said in a disgusted voice. We're stuck in a rural area near Murphy, staying with a couple who're pro-life and live quietly, but they're dull as dishwater. Our dog Trumpet is smarter than they are."

"I'm sorry to hear that," King said, showing an appropriate amount of sympathy. He wondered where she was going with her complaining. It can't be anything good, he thought.

"Are you on their phone?"

"No, it's a burner. It's safe."

King had his Blowing Rock, Gastonia and Charlotte offices swept for electronic bugs every week, so he felt secure when he took sensitive calls.

"Have you stayed in their house, out of sight?" he asked.

"Mostly. We've gone camping a few times in the Smoky Mountains, but we've got good aliases. And both of us have changed our hair color and cut."

"You know you need to stay inside. There's still a big manhunt on for you guys."

"I know. I'm calling because we heard the FBI was asking about us a couple of counties away. I don't like to think of them working their way out here."

That information gave King a panicky feeling, but he quickly tried to sound reassuring.

"Well, that's unfortunate. They're probably just covering their bases again, since they didn't find you right away."

"Maybe," Ceil said. "What are you going to do about it?"

King was dismayed. He hadn't played an active role in the bombing, but he'd sure as hell had kept himself informed. Now was the time to distance himself–again.

"Ceil, you know I can't have any connection with the venture because I'm a spiritual leader and the new state's governor. You had several wealthy people in Charlotte step up to give you money and other help." He had a feeling that his words wouldn't go over particularly well.

"Only because you told them to. If we go down, we'll take you with us."

"I don't respond to threats," King said. "But your sponsors can find you another place to live–probably in South Carolina. Give them a few days or a week. Call me back from a safe phone."

She slammed the phone down, a gesture that increased his disquiet.

King called Rob, who was down the hall in the lieutenant governor's wing.

"We've got a problem," he told Rob. "Let's go out to the picnic area and I'll bring you up to date."

They walked out the front door and wound their way to the back of the property, which was adorned with bare trees, big pots that held flowers in the spring, benches and picnic tables. It was too early for the lunch crowd, so they had the place to themselves. In early January, it wasn't too cold, but the wind was whipping in from the mountains. They sat at a picnic table and whispered.

King related the gist of his conversation with Ceil, including the threat she'd made.

"Let's move them right away to one of the small houses in South Carolina, probably the Crosby house," King said. "It's empty and out of the way."

"I know the one," Rob said. "It's the small fishing cabin, right? They won't like it. Maybe the time has come for a more permanent solution."

"Remember my position. I'm governor and the pastor of an enormous church and can't be part of anything potentially dangerous or scandalous. But I don't enjoy being threatened."

He felt torn between his genuine concern for the Montgomerys and his strong desire to protect himself. He thought Rob understood.

"Sure," Rob said. "Don't worry about it. It'll all work out in the end."

CHAPTER 41

No one, not even King, knew about Rob's secret weapon: two young men he'd borrowed from the Texas Secession Army for a week. Bubba Forrest was a crack sharpshooter, and his brother Junior possessed the brain for planning that Bubba lacked. Together, they were a deadly team Rob could count on to do many distasteful tasks.

As lieutenant governor, Rob felt he needed to focus on state government, rather than bringing his enemies down. That didn't mean he'd turned over a new leaf on necessary killings—he just couldn't take the risk of doing them himself. Besides, he believed in the gravitas of the office and thought that performing such acts was beneath him.

He and King had a complicated relationship about how to deal with enemies of the new government and God's Gift Church. Rob knew that King was frantic with worry about the potential damage Ceil and Rad Montgomery could do, even though their claims to King were overblown. Rob believed King wanted him to take drastic action, though it went unspoken. Because he felt it gave him more power over King, Rob didn't mind his role as a fixer. He also had more resources than King.

Junior and Bubba were prime examples. As the two brothers stood before him, Rob marveled at their looks. They were both built like enormous tree trunks with colossal heads, red faces, and small blue eyes. They were two years apart but looked more like twins. Better still, there was nothing they wouldn't do for money or their cockeyed philosophy.

"Hey, boss," Junior said with a drawl. "We miss you down in West Texas. When you comin' back?" Bubba nodded his agreement with his brother. Junior did most of the talking for them both.

"Oh, I may be gone for quite a while," Rob said. "I'm lieutenant governor of this new state, which is a big deal. I just need some help from time to time and I remembered you guys."

How could I forget these two idiots? Their IQ together probably doesn't exceed 120. But they're born killers and glad to take direction from a former leader of the Texas secession movement, Rob reflected.

He knew he should pity Junior and Bubba, whose mother had left them as toddlers. An alcoholic father in West Texas had raised them, often leaving them to forage for food. The one useful thing he'd taught them was how to shoot any kind of gun. That knowledge drew them to the secession army, where their expertise was in demand. For hired killers, they had one oddity. They loved cats and rescued any strays they could find. People brought them cats and knew who to seek if they wanted a cat. Nobody knew how many cats they had, but their beat-up trailer smelled indescribably awful.

Rob gave them a rural address near Murphy in far Westcarolina, where he knew that Ceil and Rad Montgomery were staying.

"Watch the house for a day or two to observe their daily routine," he said. "The Latimers, the couple they're living with, go to work every weekday morning, leaving the Montgomerys home alone. That's when you'll want to strike. Remember, do a quick survey of their room for briefcases, documents, and any other paperwork you can take with you."

"We got it," Junior said.

Rob handed them a box with a new burner phone inside.

"Call me when you're done over there," he said. "I'll want to know briefly how it went as you hightail it back to West Texas. At some point soon, I'll have another assignment for you."

They stood there, silent before Rob, till he got the message.

"Sorry," he said. He rummaged through his bottom desk drawer, came up with an envelope stuffed with cash, and handed it to Junior.

"There's $5,000 in there," he told them. "You get the other $5,000 after it's done. There might be a second assignment later. I haven't really decided yet."

"You also said you'd give us mileage," Junior said. "This couple doesn't have any children, right?"

"No children. They were the ones who bombed the abortion pill factory near here. You might have heard about it."

"Yeah. A righteous cause. You sure they need killing?"

"Positive. It was a secret mission and now they're threatening to talk about it."

Both nodded vigorously. They'd been well-schooled in secrecy, the requirement for such work.

"Okay, we'll leave right after lunch. Is there a Popeye's near here?" Junior asked. "Love their fried chicken."

"I wouldn't know." Rob basically stuck to a Mediterranean diet, believing that it would preserve his healthy physique.

"Well, we'll probably talk to you the day after tomorrow. It will take all day to get there. Tomorrow, we'll surveil them and on Wednesday we'll probably carry out the mission very early if the time is right," Junior said. Bubba vigorously nodded.

"After it's accomplished, you'll need to drive quickly to West Texas, where nobody can lay a hand on you. That's still true, right?"

At the mention of their Nation of Texas secessionist territory, both men removed their cowboy hats for a moment, a gesture of allegiance formerly reserved for the Alamo.

"Yeah. We'll be untouchable."

Rob spent the next two days on tenterhooks, wondering if the two soldiers of the secessionist Army were up to the task. Late morning on the third day, he saw on the news wires that someone had shot and killed the Montgomerys and the Latimers. No one was in custody and the government had no suspects. The FBI was investigating the scene of the four deaths.

Rob was aghast. He hadn't okayed the killing of the Latimers and wondered what had happened. Usually, the Forrests strictly obeyed orders.

Finally, the phone rang.

"Tell me how it went down." He asked Junior, not bothering to wait for them to slowly unspool the story. Anxiety consumed him. So many things could have gone wrong.

"Mission accomplished," Junior said with pride. "Unfortunately, the Latimers had apparently forgotten something and came back as we were checking out the Montgomerys' room. We had to shoot them, too. We left them inside the house and the Montgomerys in the garden."

"Where are you?"

"On the road, a few hours from Marfa." Marfa, a former arts colony town, now was the epicenter of the secessionist movement. Tourists never went there because they knew that the violent secessionist army held it.

"Tell me more."

"We did what you said. It took us the rest of Monday to get there. On Tuesday, we surveilled the house all day. The Latimers left in the early morning and came home that afternoon from work, but the Montgomerys didn't show their faces.

"On Wednesday, we caught a break. Soon after the Latimers left, the Montgomerys came out the back door. We guessed they were going to work in the big garden in the backyard. We shot them both in the back of their heads, checking to make sure they were dead. They never knew what hit them. The Latimers came back unexpectedly–you already know the end of that story."

"After we shot them and made sure they were dead, we skedaddled."

"Did you see anyone, or did anyone see you?"

"I don't think so," Junior said.

"What do you mean?"

"Well, a couple of cars passed us, going on the gravel road toward the house, but I highly doubt they'd remember us."

Rob bit his lip, resisting the temptation to shout. Their old truck was white with monster wheels. Not the sort of vehicle two assassins should have.

He heard strange noises in the background.

"I hear noise. What is it?"

"We rescued a mama cat and her four kittens from the side of the road in Texas," Junior said. "They are really cute solid black kitties. We'll find good homes for them or keep them."

Rob tried not to show his disdain. He hated cats and most other animals. He couldn't stand to be around the filthy things.

"Boss, do we get a bonus for shooting four people instead of two?" Junior asked.

"No." Rob practically yelled into the phone. "Shooting the Latimers was a mistake that could have jeopardized the entire mission. Surely you see that."

"Okay, okay," Junior said in an injured tone. "I thought you'd be happy."

"Never mind," Rob said. "Just keep driving. Make sure nobody follows you. Don't stop anywhere until you get home."

His mind still whirled around the mission. The more he thought about it, the more the shooting of the Latimers made sense. Who knows what they would've told the FBI under duress? But he had no intention of paying the Forrests extra.

"Thanks, boss," Junior said. "Just call when you decide it's time for the other one."

CHAPTER 42

A month later, on a cold, windy February morning, Annie and Jim sat in her cubicle for a planning session that lasted nearly two hours. They wanted to figure out their next steps in investigating the shooting deaths of the two abortion pill factory bombers and their host couple in rural Westcarolina.

Annie and Jim were stumped, but they understood they weren't the only ones. Through their sources in the FBI, they learned that the federal agency's probe had yielded no answers so far. Federal agents had combed the far end of Westcarolina for anyone who might have seen the shootings or anything suspicious. So far, they hadn't found a single person who either knew anything or was willing to talk. That wasn't out of the ordinary in the border region, where many locals hated the federal government and kept their own counsel as much as possible.

Annie firmly believed that lieutenant governor Rob Ryland was behind it. She knew he had a spotless alibi that day, appearing before a God's Gift Church high-level committee that morning. Jim had talked to Rob following the meeting, looking for possible news. Rob had been forthcoming, telling Jim all about the planning efforts for a church mosquito eradication campaign in Africa.

That meeting was suspicious, because Rob's dealings with church officials were rare. As lieutenant governor, he spent most of his time on Westcarolina business. He wasn't exactly a stalwart proponent of any church. Annie thought perhaps Rob had planned his alibi carefully.

She wondered how much the awful night years ago when Rob had raped her had colored her suspicions of him. Since she'd learned that he'd settled in Westcarolina, she had tried to avoid even the sight of him. She hated his nasty, suggestive comments and the terrible memories they brought back. Jim luckily enjoyed covering the lieutenant governor's office because Rob was energetic about changes, which produced good stories.

She'd visited King at his offices twice since the murders and had observed him any sign of culpability when she mentioned the four dead co-conspirators. But he seemed to react normally. She knew that he also had an alibi, holding a well-publicized Gastonia meeting that day with some out-of-state officials on cannabis distribution. Annie had attended part of the meeting and had even written a story.

There was no way either of the two leaders could have gotten to the rural area near the town of Murphy. The house where Ceil and Rad Montgomery had been living was so isolated that it was no wonder the feds couldn't find them, even after a months-long hunt.

She thought it would have been easy for Rob, probably thinking that murder was beneath his exalted state, to hire someone to do his dirty work. She'd told Jim to observe his actions, as she would without talking to him about anything they might find.

Annie and Jim were reaching the end of another fruitless meeting when she checked her laptop for incoming messages. Instead, she saw a breaking news bulletin from the Raleigh newspaper that shocked her.

A bizarre murder had claimed the lives of Sam Waller, the longtime state senator, and Ike Hinton, the minority leader of the House, on their way to the Outer Banks.

The killings, on a quiet stretch of rural roadway, were being investigated by the FBI. The car, going at high speed, had left the highway and hit a culvert. A second vehicle had stopped. Waller and Hinton, who were apparently slightly injured, probably expected the motorists to help them. They had rolled down the car windows. Instead, someone fatally shot the two legislators. Eventually, another motorist stopped and called 911.

Waller and Hinton, close friends who frequently traveled together, were heading to Rodanthe, a slim stretch of land below Kill Devil Hills. In the past few weeks, multiple houses had collapsed into the ocean there. The dramatic examples of beach erosion had led to a highly publicized fact-finding mission by Waller, Hinton and a few other state legislators.

"Oh my gosh," Annie said. "I liked them so much when they came to see you at the office that day."

"It's a terrible loss for North Carolina," Jim said. "They were wonderful guys, among the most effective legislators in the General Assembly."

"They were also the biggest critics of Westcarolina and its leadership," Annie said. "I remember their TV interview the day King announced the new policies on tobacco and cannabis. They'd threatened to get their fellow legislators to rescind their approval of Westcarolina. Wonder if the accident had anything to do with those threats?"

"Yeah, I feel the same way," Jim said. "But I don't think King or even Rob would have the nerve to tangle with legislators."

"Should we check in with our FBI sources?" Annie said. She felt sad, and fearful. She planted the blame squarely on Rob, who could certainly arrange it. But what if King had conspired with Rob to kill their legislative enemies? In her heart, she believed that King was a good man who had the morals and judgment not to get involved with any plots to hurt or kill anyone. She also thought maybe she wanted to believe it so much that she was suspending her reporter's judgment.

"Sure."

Jim called a longtime source, a friendly FBI special agent, and spent a half hour talking to him. He hung up the phone and turned to Annie.

"My source said that the agency is investigating who was involved in the accident with Waller and Hinton. There were two sets of tire marks where their car left the road, showing that a car behind them may have forced them off the road and into the ditch."

"Right now, that's just a theory."

Annie thought for a moment before speaking.

"That's pretty brazen. I know it was early morning, and an isolated stretch of the highway where the murder happened, but that's taking a big chance that no one would have seen anything out of the ordinary."

"Yeah, more and more, I think that hired killers were involved in Waller and Hinton's car accident and the shooting of the Montgomerys and Latimers," Jim said.

"Who hired them and from where?" Annie mused. "I would imagine that Rob still has contacts in the Nation of Texas secessionist army."

"That sounds plausible," Jim said. "That's for us to investigate. It doesn't seem that the FBI is making any headway in solving either of those crimes."

"I haven't talked to King in a few days. I think it's time to call him."

Annie called his private number, and he picked up the phone immediately.

"Hi, Annie. What can I do to help you today?"

"Have you seen the North Carolina news in the last couple of hours?"

"You're probably talking about Waller and Hinton's accident on their way to the Outer Banks."

"Yes, some officials don't believe it was an accident, that there may have been a second car involved."

"That's terrible," King said. "What's their theory?"

"That a mysterious car may have run theirs off the road."

"Well, they were certainly our worst enemies in the legislature, but it's horrible if someone tried to kill them. Annie listened closely as he thought for a moment and spoke in what she thought of as an incredulous tone.

"You don't think I had anything to do with it, do you?"

"No, King, but I can't think of anyone who'd benefit more if they weren't on the scene."

"Please believe me, Annie. I would never do anything to hurt them. I liked them and thought I could bring them around to become supporters of Westcarolina."

"I want to believe you, King. But you don't have to convince me. I'm sure there will be questions from the FBI."

"And I will answer them. But your opinion is worth more to me than any others. I hope you know that."

"I hear you, King. But for your own good, that's not the way you should be thinking right now."

CHAPTER 43

The day after the legislators' fatal accident, King asked Rob to come to his office. He waited with trepidation for Rob to walk across the cavernous living room at the Blowing Rock mansion to King's wing.

King had always found it helpful to have Rob nearby, though both had separate suites of offices now. The two still worked closely together, though not as much as they did before King nominated Rob for the post of lieutenant governor. According to Westcarolina's proposed legislative rules, that was King's prerogative, at least for now. Sometimes he worried that he'd created a monster.

Today was one of those days, which was why he needed to talk with Rob posthaste. The lieutenant governor arrived fifteen minutes later. King believed that Rob intentionally made him wait to show his increased power since the time when Rob was his top aide.

"Hey, King," Rob said, shaking the governor's hand warmly. If he had any inkling that he was being called on the carpet, he hid it well. King motioned for him to sit.

King thought Rob looked as physically fit as usual, his Westcarolina athletic shirt showing off his muscles, built up by long hours in the mansion's gym. But his face looked careworn with a few wrinkles, like he'd had a few too many sleepless nights and tension-filled days. His voice also sounded slightly nervous. He spoke quickly, his Texas drawl not as drawn out as usual.

"Let's talk about the Montgomery killings, which it seems that you ordered without getting the go-ahead from me," King said with barely suppressed anger.

"That's not quite correct," Rob answered.

"When did I say to kill that couple? We talked about getting them to a safer place, specifically the fishing cabin in South Carolina."

"And I said it might be time to consider a more permanent solution," Rob replied with a defensive manner. "As I recall, you didn't tell me not to do it. On the contrary. You seemed relieved by the suggestion."

"I thought you'd check in with me before it came time to decide what to do. Suddenly, four people are dead, including the Latimers, who never did a thing to deserve it."

"The Latimers, unfortunately, were collateral damage," Rob said.

"They came home from work unexpectedly. My two guys had already dispatched Ceil and Rad and were searching their room for anything incriminating."

"Who are those guys?" King asked with consuming curiosity. His work as an evangelical minister and now governor of a new state hardly had included any contacts with professional assassins.

"In West Texas, there are a couple of young men working as hired guns. Despite being not very intelligent, the guys excel at whatever tasks they are given. They seem to thrive on breaking the law and causing chaos. They're back in Texas now."

"What did that criminal act cost?"

"About $10,000 in all. Those bozos wanted me to pay them extra for the unauthorized killings of the two extra people and I gave them a harsh no. I went into the slush fund you and I control. The amount I gave them barely put a dent in it." Rob said. "You see we avoided a heap of trouble by getting rid of the Latimers. The feds would have found them and picked their brains for months. That couple could have implicated some people who have bankrolled the Montgomerys. You know the ones I'm talking about—the rich couples that live in the wealthy suburbs of Charlotte."

"Perhaps," King said. "But I won't have this come back on me. I will not pay for someone else's mistakes."

He thought it better not to accuse Rob by name. He'd assumed that the lieutenant governor would be penitent and apologetic, but he'd not foreseen the newly emboldened Rob.

His former sidekick refrained from pointing out that King had helped to enlist the help of the high rollers in Charlotte.

"Neither you nor I will accept the blame."

"Well, you better be right about this," King said, slightly mollified.

"Let's move on to the deaths of Ike Hinton and Sam Waller," he added. "I did not know of that, and I'm not gullible enough to think it was an accident."

Rob pondered for a moment before explaining that they had driven off the road, possibly to make a small adjustment to the car, and unknown criminals shot them. "It was early in the morning, and they were driving to the Outer Banks on a deserted stretch of road. It was a crime of opportunity."

"Yeah, but I heard the feds are looking at evidence of two sets of tire tracks at the scene. They could have been deliberately run off the road, perhaps by people who had researched them and their upcoming schedules."

"Where did you hear that?"

"Annie Price mentioned it in a phone call."

Rob laughed shortly, and King thought his face looked bitter.

"Do you get all your information from that bitch?"

King bristled. He was tired of Rob's carping about Annie.

"Don't talk that way about her. She has a lot of inside sources."

"Never mind. I don't see how those deaths could be tied to us."

"Why did you do it? Did you hire the same two assassins?"

"Of course. Hinton and Waller posed an enormous threat to us. If you recall, they said they were going to get the legislature to decertify Westcarolina."

King hadn't known for sure that Rob was involved with the car deaths of Hinton and Waller. But he had suspected that the mishap was no accident. Now that Rob had admitted his culpability, he could use it as a weapon against King, if need be.

"Keep an eye on that situation," he told Rob. "And let me know if you hear anything new."

"Speaking of new, I've got an idea that would energize your church members and all of those ultra-conservative people in the far west around Murphy."

"Yeah, shoot." Oops, I used some unfortunate wording there, King thought.

"You know about the pro-choice bus? It leaves from Asheville every Monday to take women from Westcarolina to Charlotte for abortions. It would be easy to find someone to tamper with it and send it off a cliff, or at least disable it for major repairs."

King looked at Rob in horror.

"Are you nuts? We're sweating the other stuff, and you want to kill a dozen women getting abortions? Even our conservative church members would be horrified."

King couldn't believe what he was hearing. For the first time, he suspected that Rob had at least some qualities in common with psychopaths. He didn't seem to care about potentially snuffing out the lives of a large contingent of women and their fetuses. Under the handsome exterior was an ugly set of morals.

"Easy, King. Plenty of the pro-life crowd would love it."

"Please say you'll abandon that idea, Rob."

"Oh, all right. But there are lots of situations where we could change things, especially with Hinton and Waller gone."

CHAPTER 44

Annie and Jake were reading the papers at the table in their spacious kitchen when Jake's cell phone rang. He picked it up, gave her a strange look and said he'd take it in his study. A couple of minutes later, she heard him chuckling at someone he called Honey.

Annie didn't wait to hear more. She stomped upstairs past Anna's room and into their large bedroom with the king-size bed and sumptuous furnishings. Without really caring what she wore, she quickly dressed in black slacks and a white shirt. She went into her massive closet and grabbed her leather jacket with such force that the hanger clanged to the floor. She stopped to check on Anna, who was sleeping peacefully in her crib. As she hurried downstairs, Jake was still on the phone. She heard him tell the person on the line that he'd call back later. Her pride kept her from asking why he was on the phone to someone he called Honey.

"I have to leave now for the appointment with King in Gastonia," she called out, keeping her voice even. "You can still stay here for the next few hours, right?" As he knew, their babysitter was taking the morning off.

"Of course."

She wondered if the call had anything to do with their upcoming trip. He'd arranged for her and Anna to fly to Austin the next weekend to see his kids and introduce them to their new half-sister. It would be Anna's first plane ride and out-of-town weekend, and Annie was half excited, half dreading it. Luckily, the plane ride was slightly more than a two-hour flight, so maybe Anna would sleep through it. Jake, leaving a day early for work, would miss that milestone. She didn't really think he cared. That was the drawback to marrying a man who already had children. With the fourth child, very little was new and exciting. Although, to be fair, he seemed to enjoy the signs of their baby growing and changing. Was it all just an act?

Jake's latest phone call mystified Annie. He'd gotten several mysterious calls in the past few days. He'd sounded flirtatious, which meant, of course, that they were from women. She felt disheartened, but she would not give in to her curiosity. Was Jake's behavior with women going to hurt her the rest of their married life? Could she put up with it? Did she even want to?

His appreciation of women had drawn her because he so extravagantly complimented her looks and practically everything she did. When he had first paid attention to her, she was thrilled. He satisfied her needs at some mysterious level she didn't quite understand. He was a fantastic lover and an entertaining friend.

There had been no incidents that had really bothered her since Maggie Mahaffey, the queen of pink, had showed up unannounced at his office. Jake had accused Annie of being needlessly jealous of his attention to Maggie and she'd not mentioned the younger woman since. But she wondered what he did on those twice-a-month solitary trips to Austin. Of course, he spent time with his three children there and at the law partnership office, but what did he do in the off hours?

She was in a black mood by the time she reached the state administration building in Gastonia. She could understand why King preferred to work at his mountain house. The red building with its small windows today looked completely unwelcoming and anonymous. She sighed as she parked her car and got out. She wasn't in the frame of mind to interview anyone, since it took considerable energy to wring information out of people. But she'd arranged it, so she'd follow through. Luckily, once she went into reporter mode, she usually forgot her own troubles.

His secretary waved her on and she walked into his office on the first floor. He stood up to greet her and Annie thought his face changed from worried to delighted. She was sure her face brightened, too. Here was someone who really liked her and as far as she could tell, didn't flirt with other women. Well, not in front of her, anyway.

"Hi, Annie. Thanks for coming by. I've got a tricky situation and I'd like to share it with you."

"Okay. What's going on?"

"You know about the church's residential sales program? I think you've asked about it. I can't deny that the small houses we built in the Gastonia area were expensive for the young people who bought them. But people from God's Gift flocked to the houses, so we kept building more. Now, with interest rates rising and adjustable-rate mortgages going up, the homeowners are upset. They're paying hundreds of dollars more than some can afford and they're blaming the church, especially me."

"King, unfortunately, that sounds perfectly understandable. I'd blame you, too. How many have you—or the church—sold?"

He was silent for a moment, with a guilty expression on his face. Annie thought he must be adding up the sales in his head.

"I think it's probably about 2,000 in five new subdivisions. That's over a period of about seven years. Land was cheap, and it seemed like the ideal investment."

He had the grace to look ashamed for exploiting church members, Annie thought.

"What happens next?"

"The day after tomorrow, the homeowners' associations have asked me to talk at a big protest meeting. Of course, I told them yes, but I'm not sure how I'm going to handle it. What do you think I should do?"

"You're asking me, who will have to report on it? I can't give you advice, King, except to say that you should do the right thing, whatever your mind and your heart tell you."

"Thank you, Annie. That's great advice from the person I most respect."

That this man cared so much and seemed so eager to get her opinions brought tears to Annie's eyes. It was such a contrast to the doubts she'd felt that morning with Jake.

"What are you crying about, Annie?" King asked, coming around the desk and clasping her hands.

"Oh, the usual," she said, trying to slough it off. "Just some issues with Jake."

"I can empathize. My life with Claire is one big issue. I take it you've heard that she's unfaithful?"

"Yeah, I've heard that. But I'd never have mentioned it unless you brought it up first."

"It's the one constant in my marriage. Usually, every year or even every few months, Claire will find a new man with whom to have an extended affair. I've suggested couples' counseling or even a divorce, but she doesn't want either. I can tell she has another new lover, but I have no idea who it might be or what she really feels. It never stops hurting." His voice trailed off, echoing his misery.

"Can't you file for divorce? It seems like you have plenty of grounds and the situation makes you miserable."

"Until now, I have had no reason to take that step," he said, looking into her eyes.

"I love you, Annie. I'd like to be your lover and marry you when I can arrange it."

King's bald statement shocked Annie, as it had seemed obvious for the past few months. On one hand, his feelings moved her. The possibility that their relationship was coming to a head alarmed her. She gave herself a minute to think, picking out her words carefully.

"I have feelings for you, King, but I'm not sure what they are. They may just arise from the fact that I'm disappointed in my marriage right now."

His answer was to squeeze her hands. She knew that with the slightest encouragement, he would kiss her passionately.

"Even though Jake could be cheating on me, I will not cheat on him. We married in good faith and our little girl needs her father. Now, let's go back to me being a reporter and you answering my questions."

CHAPTER 45

The next day, Annie wrote a brief article about buyers' growing dissatisfaction with the God's Gift Church home building program. She intended to use the story, published Tuesday, to preview King Avery's press conference in Gastonia on Wednesday.

She knew the Gastonia couple she sought regularly for comment had bought one of the houses. Barbara Aydlette was a nurse, her husband Bob, a firefighter, and they had two young children. They were faithful church members who'd been excited to leave their rented apartment.

"We thought we were so lucky to get a house," Barbara Aydlette said when Annie called. "But now, I wish we'd never bought one in the church's development. We have a leaking roof and warped floors. Since the interest rate went up, we've really struggled with money."

Annie interviewed other homeowners who'd bought into one of the five residential neighborhoods the church had built over seven years. Most of the families she talked to felt cheated, and many were extremely angry about it.

They listed two types of problems. They hadn't fully understood the terms of an adjustable-rate mortgage, which went up as interest costs increased. The other complaint was shoddy construction, which echoed most of the Aydlettes' problems.

The construction issues surprised Annie, especially because she thought the church would have been more careful to find reputable builders for the houses. The new homes were mostly bought by young church members. Many would be at King's press conference.

On Wednesday, Annie arrived early at the unfinished subdivision in Gaston County where he was to talk. She looked it over carefully.

The homes were two-story "snout houses," with the garage's entrance in the front, or small, one-story ranches. The builder had mostly alternated the two styles on each street. All were frame with stone accents. She thought it looked like a cookie-cutter subdivision that might be the best those first-time homeowners could afford. In each front yard, the builders had planted a lone oak tree.

King was to speak in front of a one-story ranch with four other unfinished houses down the street. Soon, cars were parking on that street and three others. Annie had noticed another car parked on the next street earlier that morning. They must have really wanted to get here early, she thought.

King arrived with just one aide to help him set up a sound system. He looked nervous but determined. Annie went up to him to say hello.

"I'm glad you came," he said. "I've been thinking a lot about what you said. I'm going to try to do the right thing, instead of making excuses."

"That's good, King. I talked to a lot of folks about this, and they bought the houses here because they trusted the church. Now they feel that the church has broken that trust."

She was glad that she apparently had been a positive influence on him but didn't want to make a habit of meddling. Sometimes she struggled to keep her objective role as reporter with King. He so eagerly sought her advice on a variety of issues, which flattered her.

It was time for the press conference to begin. Besides Annie, there were reporters from several area TV stations and about a dozen newspapers from all over the South.

King was representing only the church today, but his actions would affect public opinion about his governor's role. More than a hundred homeowners awaited King's opening speech and Annie saw Rob hovering in the background. Of course, trouble drew him like a magnet, she thought sourly.

She could feel the crowd softening as King spoke about the church's desire to house its younger couples. He apologized for the difficulties most had experienced with structural issues.

He fielded questions for nearly an hour before announcing that the church had set up a fund worth $15 million to help homeowners with escalating house payments and damage caused by builders.

He was explaining more about the fund when Annie heard several loud cracking noises. They sounded like rifle shots, perhaps from a house farther down the street. She looked at King and was horrified to see a rapidly spreading bloodstain on his white shirt. He fell on the grass and was ominously quiet. Annie could hear his aide calling 911.

The frightened crowd went wild, with many screaming, running, or seeking shelter in their cars. Some drove away quickly; others hid behind the outdoor walls of half-finished houses. Annie looked far beyond the area where the crowd had congregated, but she couldn't see any suspects. Pressing herself against the wall of the nearest house, she waited for police and an ambulance for King. There were no further shots. She doubted whether a sharpshooter cared about injuring anyone else. She was sure that the shots targeted King.

Who would want to hurt him, a basically good person who tried so hard to please people? She wondered if any of the angry homeowners had tried to kill him. That seemed too much like a drastic step.

Then there was Rob. Had his desire for more power gotten out of hand? She had to remind herself that she was hardly objective about that terrible man.

She heard a siren, and an ambulance drove up. Several paramedics got out and went into frenzied action. One quickly checked King's pulse. He opened his eyes. "He's alive. Let's load him into the ambo," a paramedic said.

She could see two working to stanch the bleeding and inserting an oxygen line. A third worker came out of the ambulance and said, "Is Annie Price here? He wants to talk to you--but make it fast."

Annie quickly climbed into the back of the ambulance where King lay on a stretcher, looking white, weak and dazed.

He held out his cold hand, and Annie took it, rubbing the warmth from her own hand into it.

"Stay with me," she urged. "Don't give up."

"I love you, Annie Price. Always remember that. You made me a better person."

"I care very much about you, King Avery. You're a good man. Don't leave me."

He smiled at her but winced in pain. Shocked, she watched the light slowly leave his eyes.

"He's gone," one paramedic said gently. "We need to transport him to the hospital for a doctor to pronounce him dead. Can you tell these people who are still here?"

Annie nodded and made a low-key announcement to the couple of dozen people who were still there. Some started weeping and others talked in low voices.

Annie could barely speak without crying. This was the man who'd been the entire focus of her reporting life for nearly a year. He'd kissed her softly one day and danced with her when she was heavily pregnant. He rushed her to the hospital when she went into labor and stayed there until Jake came. They'd shared jokes and stories about their youth. The entire scene was so unreal. How could he be dead?

But there was no time to cry. This was arguably the biggest story of her career. She quickly called the office and reported everything she'd seen—minimizing her own role—to an editor taking dictation. He urged her to stay on the scene for a while, questioning police who'd swarmed on to the church's property.

"Let me speak to Jim," she said urgently. Her reporting partner came on the line, and she told him to call Rob, now the governor-apparent for the state of Westcarolina. He'd apparently left the scene but carried his cell around all the time. She and Jim would divide up the work, but she couldn't stomach talking to Rob right now.

Six hours later, with Annie back in the newsroom, they'd met all their deadlines for the next day. An impressive package about King and the shocking events of the day was online and would be published with updates in the next day's paper's paper. Unanswered were plenty of questions–who'd shot King, why, where had the shooter hidden, and more.

Annie had checked in with Jake earlier to tell him she was okay, and she called him back.

"I'm coming home soon. The night crew will take over checking in with the cops all night. I've done the best I can do."

"I know you have, honey," he said gently. "Anna is asleep. Come home and I'll have a glass of Chardonnay waiting."

"Okay."

Annie went to the newspaper's garage, got into her car, and for the first time that day, sobbed.

CHAPTER 46

Annie cried in her car for a while before she looked at her watch. It was nearly 11 p.m. and Jake would be waiting. She needed to get home, but she was still having a hard time sorting out her tangled emotions. She stopped at a service station to repair the damage to her tear-stained face.

She went in one superstation, past the stale coffee, roasting hot dogs, down the aisle full of candy and found the ladies' room. Inside, she inspected her face, and it was even more red and swollen than she thought it would be. Talk about ugly crying, she thought. She bathed her face in cold water, dried it, powdered it and reapplied her lipstick. Jake deserved at least a semblance of normalcy.

She parked at their mega-house, used her key to open the door, and there was Jake. He took one look at her face and enveloped her in his muscular arms.

"Oh, baby," he said, rocking her as he hugged her. "I know you've had a terrible day. I'll get you a glass of the good Chardonnay and you can tell me about it. Anna is still asleep, so we have plenty of time."

She sank into the leather sofa in their den, and he brought her a glass of wine and sat beside her. He had a glass half-filled with Knob Creek to sip as they talked.

"Thanks, honey," she said automatically. "I'm sorry I'm such a mess. This is the third shooting I've witnessed, and though I was the one who got shot in the last one, this was the most shocking."

Her mind flew back to the Texas Hill Country a few years ago when she was wounded while investigating the illegal adoption ring. Somehow, that wasn't as horrific as the killing of King she'd seen today.

"The reporter on the evening TV news out of Charlotte said you were the last to talk with King," Jake said. She could tell that he was measuring his words.

"He wanted to say goodbye. I held his hand and told him to hang on a little longer. But he died as I watched him. It was wrenching." She'd decided she couldn't tell Jake–or anyone else–that they'd exchanged words of love before he passed away. Was it duplicitous? Yes, but she just couldn't hurt him that way. She hadn't told King she loved him–just that she cared. Even in that dire situation, she wanted to be true to Jake.

"He'd asked the paramedics to bring me into the van. I guess I was the only person there who knew him well enough to come to his deathbed. He knew he was dying and didn't have long."

Tears slipped from Annie's eyes again, but she could regain her composure.

"Did he say he loved you? That's probably what I would have done in his shoes." Jake's face looked watchful and searching.

"Yes." she said simply. Was Jake psychic or just probing a sticky situation? How far could she go with him?

"Annie, I won't ask what you said, but I know you had feelings for him. You wanted to get out of the house and interview him as often as you could."

"I can't deny that he meant something special to me, but I was never unfaithful to you. I never told him I loved him." She sat up straighter on the sofa and locked eyes with him. His gaze was unflinching as he replied.

"As I learned in my first marriage, there are lots of ways to be unfaithful. I can't and won't let that happen to us. We have a baby to raise, and I love you dearly. Do you still love me?"

His words and his intensity took her aback. This wasn't the Jake she saw every day, irreverent, bawdy, and laughing at life's absurdities.

"Of course I love you. You've been in my heart for years. I just get consumed by doubt when you go to Austin. I know Maggie is prowling around you, and probably many other women. You're handsome and funny and a babe magnet. Just today, I heard you on the phone calling a woman honey. How can I compete with that?"

"Annie, the woman on the phone, is an admin in our Austin headquarters. Her name is Honey, and she's arranging your surprise birthday party, which unfortunately is not a surprise anymore. As for Maggie, she's just a pest who won't go away. Yes, we had an affair before you and I married, but I never took it seriously and haven't succumbed to her far too frequent appearances in the office. Eventually, she'll meet someone and stop coming by.

"I spend my time in Austin working and seeing my kids. Period. Stop doubting me. It's destroying our relationship."

"I know, Jake, and I'll work on it. I'm committed to our marriage, and I'll do anything to make it better." She moved closer to him on the sofa, and he put his arm around her. She was relieved when he kissed her lightly.

"Okay," he said. "Let's not talk about this anymore tonight. It's painful to both of us. Besides, I want to know who killed King."

"Oh, Jake. I just know Rob Ryland was behind it. I'm betting that he hired a hitman to do it, just like he arranged the killings of the four people in the mountains and the two legislators on the coast. He's drunk with power and becoming governor will make him even more dangerous. I don't know how I can prove what he's done. I can't work with him." Her desperation was clear with each syllable. She slumped on the sofa and looked exhausted.

"Now, hold on, baby. I know what Rob did to you, and it was horrible. But it's time to let it go. You're a professional and you'll have Jim full time to help you cover him."

"Do you really think I could work with him?" Annie, so decisive, sounded timorous and overly dependent on Jake's opinion. She knew that this place of weakness came from the day she'd had.

"I think you should hold off deciding until you try to get answers on King's killing. If you resign now, Rob wins." He was as serious and emphatic as she'd ever seen him.

"I hadn't thought about it that way." She could feel her reporter's resolve kicking in.

"If you feel the least bit threatened, we'll leave. But harming a reporter is a little like attacking a law enforcement officer. The repercussions are enormous."

"I know that's true. The world's journalism establishment would revolt against him, and Rob knows that." She was becoming emboldened by Jake's words.

"Why don't we sleep on it? Jake said. "I'd like to hold you close and forget about today. See how you feel tomorrow. I will do anything you want me to do."

"Okay. I'll think about it tomorrow, as Scarlett O'Hara said. This weekend belongs to you, me and Anna."

CHAPTER 47

Rob woke abruptly from a nightmare. The people he'd killed were taunting him with promises of punishment, either from an angry God, or from the state of Westcarolina. He breathed hard and told himself it was just a meaningless dream. He'd had bad dreams since the recent death of King. The other six people whose killings he'd arranged—well, seven including his part in Henry's mountaintop demise—weren't personal friends or people he'd cared about the way he'd liked King.

He looked at the naked woman sleeping next to him in the four-poster bed where King used to sleep. Claire Avery had a gorgeous body, naked or clothed, he had to admit. But her face, without fresh makeup, showed some wear and tear. Rob guessed her age to be somewhere north of 40. He wasn't averse to dating older women, but her naked appearance belied her somewhat desperate attempt at projecting youth. The affair with King's wife had begun several months ago, initiated by her, directed by her. She was always arranging new adventures, a threesome with another woman, a foursome with a freewheeling couple, and a few other delights Rob had never experienced. He didn't think King ever suspected that Rob and Claire would betray him.

In some ways, Rob thought, he and Claire were alike—out for themselves and their own pleasures. As incredible as he found it, she'd helped arrange her husband's death by telling Rob exactly where King was going to be for his press conference. He knew King was planning to speak about the housing complaints, but he didn't know the neighborhood for the press conference until he'd asked Claire to find out. Rob and King hardly ever communicated about their schedules anymore. That'd allowed Rob to summon Bubba and Junior Forrest to do the thing they did best. Rob felt pleased that the assassination of King had gone off without a hitch, at least it appeared that way so far. A few days after the killing, he felt almost home free–that is, when he was awake.

He knew that after he plotted to dispatch Henry Fullspear by arranging his fall off the mountain, that this day would come. King had made sure that as his primary aide and partner in various schemes, he would appoint Rob as lieutenant governor to succeed Fullspear, at least until the next election. King had made a fatal mistake by thinking Rob would be grateful, but Rob was already thinking how he'd supplant King. He waited patiently while King tried all kinds of new initiatives, most of which fell flat with public criticism. He judged King to be careless in planning changes, not bothering to build enough public support.

The only policy change that'd gone smoothly was the marijuana venture, mostly because King had planned it for years. Rob would allow all tobacco products to be sold while keeping marijuana legal. There was no reason to pass up the easy tax money tobacco products provided. He didn't give a damn how many people tobacco killed each year–it was their own fault for letting themselves become addicted. Rob, as a physical fitness fanatic, smoked nothing except marijuana cigarettes and rarely had more than one beer. He didn't understand why King had been so priggish about tobacco.

Rob was also mulling how he'd separate God's Gift Church from Westcarolina. What King had been doing was not sustainable. He'd been spending part of his time as de facto head of the mega-church while charged with governing Westcarolina. King had given some of the more able pastors increased responsibilities and hired a few so-so administrators, but never could take his hands off the wheel. Rob didn't believe in all the mumbo-jumbo of that church, or any church. All he wanted from it was money and power. If King had done it right, all the Westcarolina churches, including God's Gift, would be paying taxes, and wouldn't be complaining about it, either. He had several good lawyers researching how to do this and stay out of trouble with the federal government. He'd find and take all of King's slush funds hidden in the church budget and open a Swiss bank account. He'd use that money to start a long-term account which, with any luck, would amount to at least a million dollars in his first year of governing.

Rob would find a way to monetize almost everything in Westcarolina. He'd build up its tourist industry with gambling, topless entertainment and free-flowing liquor, even some covert prostitution. Hiking, camping, canoeing, and skiing were already major draws to the state, and Rob preferred them, especially canoeing. But he thought that most tourists were fat slobs who liked a dollop of sin with their vacations.

He'd cater to the conservative tastes of the Westcarolina residents with bans on a few things like abortion, which still seemed to be a flashpoint. Rob knew that many Westcarolina women would simply go to Virginia, where there were almost no restrictions if they needed an abortion. He'd secretly invested in several abortion clinics in southwest Virginia. Women could also go to Charlotte or other N.C. cities, but they'd face more restrictions on the procedure.

There was much to be done in politics. He'd hand-picked, with King's concurrence, two fawning Republican leaders for the U.S. Senate and a few for the House. In the new state, the GOP would likely win most elections. He was facing his own election in June but had little doubt he'd win.

These thoughts swirled through his head while he admired himself in the mirror of the Blowing Rock mansion's enormous bedroom. With only his black briefs on, he could appreciate his flat stomach and muscled biceps. For his mid-thirties, he knew he looked good. Only the receding hairline of his dark brown hair looked out of place on his near-perfect body. He'd see what he could do about that after the election.

"You must like what you see. You've been preening long enough," Claire teased.

He felt startled. She went from sound asleep to fully awake—like some kind of wild animal. The analogy somehow fit because she was a tigress in bed. Truth be told, she wore him out. He could see why she and King never meshed. King had been a man of normal appetites, Rob thought. Claire, however, was closer to being a nymphomaniac. She attracted plenty of extra-marital boyfriends, but they never lasted more than a few months.

Rob didn't know how long their relationship would last. He hoped it would last long enough to gain the Blowing Rock mansion, since Claire didn't seem to love it like he did. He suspected she would try to sell it, or that she was planning to marry him, since she was taken with power. Rob had no intention of marrying Claire. He suspected that she'd tire of him and start the cycle again of endless boyfriends. He didn't think she'd be a very good governor's wife, since the gossip from her affairs would always follow her—and him. Besides, there was something crass about her that was unattractive. That she'd so easily given up her husband to assassins was scary, he thought. If they broke up, he'd better be very careful. He'd never actually told her he'd commissioned King's death, but she probably knew.

He still considered Annie Price the perfect woman, and potentially the ideal governor's wife. She was as smart a woman as he'd ever met and beautiful in her own way. She'd been a brilliant teacher during his short-lived career at the Houston Times, before he'd decided that the secessionist movement was the path to power and riches. Also, he remembered his special night with her, which she called rape, but he thought of as a wonderfully successful seduction. How would he accomplish his goal?

He could kill Jake Satterfield, that rich lawyer she'd married, but he was afraid she'd carry the torch for him. And there was the baby. As ruthless as Rob was, he'd never kill an infant.

Despite his cold-bloodedness in arranging the deaths of seven people, Rob couldn't forget them—especially King. They haunted him at night, and he was terrified he'd be unmasked. The more he tried to tell himself he'd be all right, the more those deaths lodged in his unconscious. He didn't think he'd ever be quite rid of the guilt. He'd never be the same.

CHAPTER 48

Annie was enjoying her bag lunch with Jim in the newspaper cafeteria. Two weeks after King was fatally shot, Annie was just regaining her equilibrium. She, Jake and Anna had enjoyed a week of special closeness because she'd taken some downtime for the 12-hour days she'd been working. She and Jake had taken Anna to parks, walking trails and played with her on the grass, since the weather was unusually good for winter. They'd tried new restaurants, casual ones with Anna, or fancy places for the two of them if their nanny could babysit. They had done a lot of lounging around the house and talking over glasses of wine after putting Anna to bed. Jake's sweet attention was taking some of the sting out of the traumatic events.

Because she'd been so busy with work, she felt that she'd never seen Westcarolina properly. They were planning a long trip soon to see places that particularly interested her--the resort town of Highlands; some small towns, including Murphy, near the bombers' hideout; Cherokee, where the big casino was located; and Hendersonville, because she'd heard it was charming. She wanted to climb some mountains and navigate some of the tamer rapids at Nantahala. She wanted to explore the richness of the new state.

As she and Jim shared some chocolate chip cookies she'd made for Jake, they began plotting their upcoming coverage.

"We need to divide up the Westcarolina beat for day-to-day coverage, while both of us pay special attention to what the feds are doing about King's killing," Annie said.

"Yeah, it's not like everyone has stopped in their tracks because of King's death," Jim said.

"We need to examine closely the people Rob will recommend for lieutenant governor and other key posts," Annie said. "He should make them public soon. And before we know it, it will be time for national and state elections."

Her first meeting in Blowing Rock with Rob cautiously encouraged her. He had said nothing nasty or made leering comments about raping her in Texas. Agreeing to let Jim take charge of covering him, she thought he probably felt that his innuendos weren't worthy of his new station in life. She'd cover the lieutenant governor whenever Westcarolina got one. She'd also examine Rob's policies and find news out of Westcarolina.

Her phone rang, and she picked it up, hoping it would be Jake, telling her he was fixing steaks in their outdoor kitchen tonight.

Instead, it was her best source in the FBI, which was investigating King's death. She sensed big news coming—he sounded so serious.

"Can I put you on speakerphone so that Jim can hear what you have to say?"

"Of course," Special Agent Larry Dickerson said. Jim and Larry knew and respected each other.

"Annie, I'll give you an exclusive for a couple of hours before I notify the rest of the media," he said. "We just took Governor Rob Ryland into custody for plotting the deaths of King Avery, the four anti-abortion people in the mountains, and the two legislators on the coast."

"Oh, my gosh," Annie said. "Since he was always my number one suspect, I can't say I'm too surprised, but how did you break the case?"

Dickerson told her the gist of the story. Two assassins had shot King at the governor's press conference from the second-story window of one house under construction.

When the FBI had combed the houses and examined the construction trash, special agents had found fingerprints on a plastic glass and a few cigarette butts. The window, which someone had raised for the shooting, had other fingerprints on it. The FBI had matched those prints using a national database of prior offenders.

Bubba and Junior Forrest had popped up immediately. The FBI got the Texas Rangers to pick them up in West Texas and secretly brought them back to Westcarolina. It didn't take long under intensive questioning for them to give up Rob as the mastermind of the killings. The FBI had picked up Rob without incident and he was sitting in a Gastonia jail.

"Because of the severity of the crimes, he's unlikely to get out on bail," Dickerson told her. "He'll be arraigned in court tomorrow, and I expect a crowd of journalists. Now I've got to go prepare a press release and be prepared to take a lot of media calls."

"We can't thank you enough for putting us first," Annie said. "We'll return the favor."

"I figure you've been first on the story since the beginning," the special agent said. "You deserve it."

Annie hung up the phone and looked at Jim.

"I can't take it all in," she said. "But we need to work to get something online as fast as we can." They worked furiously and in less than an hour, the gist of the stunning story was on the newspaper's website.

Annie's immediate future during the next few weeks was to chase the story as thoroughly as she could. Then there was the expedited trial a few months later, which was fascinating and attracted local, national and international media. Rob was found guilty of all charges by the jury, which meant he would likely spend the rest of his life in prison. The future of Westcarolina was up in the air. The North Carolina legislature, considering the lack of leadership and the impact of the lawsuits, was reconsidering its approval of the new state. Westcarolina was also facing renewed opposition in Congress.

Annie and Jim received the Pulitzer medal for public service. Racing to be first online with the Pulitzer announcement that day, she couldn't have foreseen how it would all unfold. Close to the end of that hectic time, Jake had raised the question: Should we move back to Texas, to Austin where Anna's sisters and brother live, and the law firm's headquarters is located? Or stay in Charlotte and she would continue to report on the uncertain future of Westcarolina? Her editors had assured her that other stories in the Charlotte area were waiting for her to investigate. She got an enhanced title–chief investigative reporter/editor.

"I won't stand in the way of your career," Jake said. "The law firm has been so impressed with the growth and business opportunities in the Charlotte area that it's probably going to establish a permanent office here that I can lead.

"I haven't told you about this yet, but there's a good chance that I might get permanent custody of the kids because of some unforeseen situations in my ex-wife's new marriage. They might eventually come to Charlotte. Would you be open to that?"

"Of course. That would be wonderful." She hoisted a glass of their finest chardonnay and smiled at Jake, her life partner and best friend.

"It sounds like Charlotte may be in our future," Jake said.

ABOUT THE AUTHOR

Nancy Stancill spent more than thirty-eight years as a newspaper reporter and editor before she began writing fiction full-time. An award-winning investigative reporter, writing in Texas, North Carolina, Virginia and California, she earned a journalism degree and a master's in creative writing.

She lives in Charlotte, North Carolina, with her husband, Len Norman, but part of her heart belongs in Pennsylvania with her son, daughter-in-law, and granddaughter.

Deadly Secrets is her fourth book and third in the Annie Price, investigative reporter, series. Her memoir, *Tall*, was her third book. When not writing, she can be found reaching items on top shelves, reading mysteries, taking long walks, and playing with her black cat, Queen Charlotte of Mecklenburg.

OTHER TITLES BY NANCY STANCILL

NOTE FROM NANCY STANCILL

Word-of-mouth is crucial for any author to succeed. If you enjoyed *Deadly Secrets*, please leave a review online–anywhere you are able. Even if it's just a sentence or two. It would make all the difference and would be very much appreciated.

Thanks!
Nancy Stancill

We hope you enjoyed reading this title from:

BLACK ROSE
writing™

<u>www.blackrosewriting.com</u>

Subscribe to our mailing list – *The Rosevine* – and receive **FREE** books, daily
deals, and stay current with news about upcoming
releases and our hottest authors.
Scan the QR code below to sign up.

Already a subscriber? Please accept a sincere thank you for being a fan of
Black Rose Writing authors.

View other Black Rose Writing titles at
<u>www.blackrosewriting.com/books</u> and use promo code
PRINT to receive a **20% discount** when purchasing.